Praise for Philip Gulley

"Philip Gulley is a Quaker pastor from Indiana with a charming sense of small-town life—and a shrewd sense of life in general... A self-deprecating narrator...he knows how to exaggerate in a witty way."
—*The Wall Street Journal*

"Gulley's work is comparable to Gail Godwin's fiction, Garrison Keillor's storytelling, and Christopher Guest's filmmaking...in a league with Jan Karon's Mitford series."
—*Publishers Weekly*

"The biggest collection of crusty, lovable characters since James Herriot settled in Yorkshire."
—*Booklist* on The Harmony Series

"The tales Philip Gulley unveils are tender and humorous... filled with sudden, unexpected, lump-in-the-throat poignancy. Through deft storytelling and his own irresistible brand of humor, [Gulley] explores the depths of the Heartland's heart. A masterpiece of Americana."
—Paul Harvey Jr.

"Philip Gulley is a beautiful writer."
—Charles Osgood, CBS *News Sunday Morning*

"Gulley is a splendid storyteller...his books abound with shrewd insights into human character."
—*Arkansas Democrat-Gazette*

"Gulley's stories get at the heart of the simple joys, stranger-than-fiction humor, and day-to-day drama of small-town life."
—*American Profile*

A Place
Called Hope

A Place
Called Hope

A Novel

PHILIP GULLEY

**CENTER
STREET**

New York   Boston   Nashville

Copyright © 2014 by Philip Gulley
Excerpt from *A Lesson in Hope* © 2014 by Philip Gulley

Center Street
Hachette Book Group
237 Park Avenue
New York, NY 10017

CenterStreet.com

Printed in the United States of America

RRD-C

First Edition: September 2014
10 9 8 7 6 5 4 3 2 1

Center Street is a division of Hachette Book Group, Inc.
The Center Street name and logo are trademarks of Hachette Book Group, Inc.

The Hachette Speakers Bureau provides a wide range of authors for speaking events. To find out more, go to www.HachetteSpeakersBureau.com or call (866) 376-6591.

The publisher is not responsible for websites (or their content) that are not owned by the publisher.

Library of Congress Cataloging-in-Publication Data

Gulley, Philip.
  A Place Called Hope : a novel / by Philip Gulley. — First edition.
     pages cm
  ISBN 978-1-4555-1980-4 (hardcover) — ISBN 978-1-4555-1981-1 (ebook).
1. Christian fiction.   I. Title.
  PS3557.U449P57 2014
  813'.54—dc23

2013050834

To Joan, my hope

Acknowledgments

No man is an island, and certainly no writer. Thank you, Steve Hanselman and Stacey Denny, my agents, for keeping me gainfully employed. I am also grateful to the good people at Center Street, especially Christina Boys, who with tact and good humor fixed my many errors. Lee and Mary Lee Comer answered the occasional legal question. The people at Fairfield Friends Meeting tolerated my absence with good cheer, most likely because my co-pastor, Jennifer Silvers, is a better preacher than me. I appreciate them, and Jennifer. Nevertheless, if there are any errors in this book, it is the fault of those who gave me poor advice. A writer is only as good as his or her advisers.

A Note to My Readers

When my children were young, my family returned to the small Indiana town where I was raised, hoping to find an environment conducive to child-rearing and book-writing. Heeding the age-old counsel to write what you know, I wrote about Sam Gardner, a Quaker pastor serving his hometown church, Harmony Friends Meeting.

Five novels and two novellas later, I moved on to theology, wanting to articulate a progressive spirituality I hoped would make a positive contribution to our society. It remains to be seen whether that has happened, but I enjoyed the opportunity, still remain committed to that goal, and continue to write and speak about that as opportunities arise.

But I sure did miss Sam Gardner and so, it appears, did many of my readers, who wrote asking of his whereabouts. Sam and I, regrettably, had lost touch with one another. He was busy with his life and I with mine. Last year, however, we reconnected at a Quaker pastors' retreat, our friendship was rekindled, and we have remained in touch ever since. I asked his permission to share his story and he agreed. (Though Sam would never say so, I think he enjoys seeing his name in print.) As it turns out, this year has been an eventful one for Sam and his family, which you will discover in the pages ahead.

A Place
Called Hope

1

Barbara Gardner had been weeping for thirty miles, staring out the car window into the distance, a pile of soggy tissues on her lap.

"It's just college," her husband, Sam, said, patting her leg. "Purdue's only ninety miles away and we'll see him next month. He'll be fine."

"Can I have Levi's bedroom?" Addison, their younger son, asked from the backseat.

"I was thinking I would use it for a home office," Sam said. "Besides, you're graduating this spring and then you'll be off to college, too."

Barbara let out a fresh wail.

She was still crying when they pulled into Harmony. It had been like this for several months—Barbara bursting into tears at the thought of their sons leaving home and Sam feeling guilty for looking forward to their departure. The thought of getting his garage back, knowing where his tools were, not finding empty milk cartons in the refrigerator, and enjoying the use of his own car was almost more than he could bear. He was, in fact, downright giddy at the prospect of launching his sons from the nest, taking a little time off work, maybe even buying a used RV and traveling a bit.

Sam Gardner was in his fourteenth year of ministry at Harmony Friends Meeting, had become adept at handling Dale Hinshaw and Fern Hampton, and had weathered the retirement of his longtime secretary, Frank, who had moved to North Carolina to be nearer his grandchildren. Once a month, Frank sent Sam a letter with pictures of his grandchildren, urging Sam to spread his wings and move south. The Quaker meeting Frank was attending needed a new pastor. Sam would be a shoo-in if he applied. However, after a few months had passed, the Quakers in North Carolina had hired a woman pastor from Iowa, whom everyone loved. Attendance at Harmony Meeting was up, giving was up, and everyone was happy. Except for Sam, who had interviewed five candidates for Frank's old job, turning down two who weren't proficient on the computer, one who didn't bathe, and Nora Nagle, the former Sausage Queen, who had retained her beauty and would cause people to speculate that she and Sam were romantically involved. He had been under intense pressure to hire Dale Hinshaw's granddaughter, Lindsey Hinshaw, who had recently, and just barely, graduated from a community college with a two-year degree in communications.

Once a month, Dale had stood in worship, during the prayer time, to update the congregation on her progress. He was of the opinion Satan had declared war against her, while Sam was of the opinion the nut didn't fall far from the tree. Their first interview had ended in tears, with Lindsey accusing Sam of not being supportive. He had said she would be responsible for preparing the weekly bulletin and she had folded, collapsing in her chair, her head in her hands, snot running down her lip, sobbing.

"I've never made a bulletin," she said. "I'm not sure I can. I don't think you understand what I've been through, the obstacles I've had to overcome."

Sam had ended the interview soon after, and was reconsidering Nora Nagle, no longer caring what a few busybodies might conjecture about their pastor and his shapely secretary working in the church basement with no one else around. But the next Sunday at church, Dale had stood during the prayer time and had asked everyone to keep Lindsey in their thoughts, that one more rejection might put her over the edge.

"She went through a time there where she was worshipping trees. It would be nice if she could find a job working with Christians," he said, looking directly at Sam.

The elders of the meeting had approached Sam after worship, suggesting he give Lindsey another interview. Dale had offered to pay half her salary for the first year, an unheard-of proposition. Eight thousand dollars! One-tenth of the church's annual budget! The Lord's will was becoming evident to the elders.

"Why don't we run her up the flagpole," Miriam Hodge suggested. "If she isn't working out after a year, you say the word and we'll cut her loose."

Miriam had recently read a book on church leadership, written by the pastor of a megachurch in Texas. She had been quoting him extensively—trite, meaningless phrases like *think outside the box* and *let's work smarter, not harder*. Sam was looking forward to the book wearing off and Miriam returning to her usual sensible self.

The next day, Nora Nagle accepted a job at the Legal

Grounds Coffee Shop on the town square, and with his options narrowed, Sam phoned Lindsey Hinshaw to tell her that after interviewing many capable candidates, he had determined she was the best of the bunch.

"I need time to think about it," she said. "Now that I have a college degree, I can't quite picture myself as a secretary. How about Director of Communications? As for the salary, I couldn't possibly live on what you're offering. I need to make at least twenty thousand dollars a year."

For someone who just the week before couldn't imagine putting together a bulletin, Lindsey had recovered nicely and was exhibiting a fair amount of pluck.

"It's a part-time job," Sam pointed out. "I'm not sure we can pay any more."

Lindsey had asked for a few days to think it over, then had gone to Dale, who upped his offer to ten thousand dollars if the church would match it, which is how Lindsey Hinshaw, who had never worked a day in her life, came to earn nearly the same amount of money as Sam Gardner, who had pastored Harmony Friends Meeting for fourteen years.

"It's all about perceived value," Miriam Hodge had told Sam. "There are lots of people who want to be ministers, but not many communication majors who want to work in the church. We have to raise your visibility, Sam. Help people see what you bring to the table."

"Well, if people don't know what I bring to the table after all these years, then I don't think raising my visibility is going to make a bit of difference," Sam had said.

"It is what it is," Miriam had said.

Sam had no idea what that meant, but Miriam had been saying it quite a bit lately. It is what it is.

In moments like these, Sam would scan the latest issue of *Quaker Life* to see which Quaker meetings were looking for pastors. It was the usual ones—dysfunctional meetings in god-forsaken towns who ran through pastors like a combine through corn, cutting them down after a season.

Lindsey Hinshaw began work the next Monday, arriving at 8:30 a.m., a half hour late. "I'll be leaving a little early today," she said. "I'm meeting a friend for lunch."

She spent the first hour sending text messages, checking her e-mail, and updating her Facebook status on the church's computer. At midmorning, Sam emerged from his office and suggested she update the church's telephone directory; he handed her a short list of new attenders.

"I'm not sure it's wise to have our names, addresses, and phone numbers in an electronic directory," Lindsey, who spent half her day on Facebook, said.

"Mostly we just use the names for our chain of prayer," Sam said. "We've done it for years with no problems."

"As the Director of Communications, I'll need to give this some thought," she said.

That evening Dale Hinshaw phoned Sam's house. "What's this about you wanting to pass out our names and addresses to complete strangers? I read about this church up in the city where these burglars got hold of a church directory and went and robbed the members' houses while they were at church. Doesn't seem all that smart to me, and I know Lindsey agrees with me."

The elders' meeting was held the next evening. Dale spent the first half hour harping about putting the church directory online.

"When you stop and think about it, what we're really doing

is making it easier for someone to break the law. Now I don't know how the rest of you feel about it, but I don't think Christians ought to be doing that. And has a church directory ever brought anyone to the Lord? I don't think so. If we're gonna be putting anything online, it oughta be something that gets folks saved."

He turned to Sam. "And I'll tell you right now, that computer makes me nervous. What happens if some wacko gets hold of it and takes us down? Shuts off our electricity and phone, takes down our grid, and here we are, sittin' ducks, locked out of our own building."

"The only things we keep on the church computer are our membership list, our giving records, and our minutes from the meetings," Sam said.

It had been a struggle to get even that much on the computer. Fern Hampton had put forth a vigorous argument for not recording donations made to the church. "It says in the Bible that when you give, you should go into a closet and do it privately. Now here we are putting it on a computer for every Tom, Dick, and Harry to see."

"I think you're confused," Sam had said. "It says prayer should be done in a closet, not giving."

"Now that makes no sense," Fern had said. "Why would you pray in a closet where no one can hear you? Dumbest thing I ever heard of."

Frank had gone ahead and recorded the donations on the computer, in a file labeled *Furnace Maintenance Schedule.*

Dale dug in, and the elders agreed to hold off updating the directory until a committee could be appointed to examine the meeting's security and what might be done to improve it.

At one time, this would have bothered Sam, but the year

before his doctor had doubled the dosage of his antidepressant. He went to the drugstore in Cartersburg, where no one knew him, to have it filled. Ministers were not supposed to be sad, depression indicating a lack of faith. Ministers were expected to have joy in the Lord and be optimistic and cheerful. The medicine had clouded his mind a bit, and caused him to nod off in the afternoon, but church meetings no longer annoyed him and his stomach had settled down. Plus, Barbara had forbid him from mentioning the words *Dale Hinshaw* and *Fern Hampton* in their home, which had calmed him somewhat, though he still had fantasies of conducting their funerals. Brief services where people stood and lied about the deceased, went downstairs to the basement and ate ham, green beans, and Jell-O, then went home inexplicably happy.

2

Lindsey Hinshaw was ending her first month as the Director of Communications for Harmony Friends Meeting and had made a thorough wreck of things, posting the wrong times for church meetings in the bulletin and neglecting to tell Sam of hospitalizations and near deaths phoned in to the office. Asa Peacock had almost died of a heart attack and had lain in the hospital in Cartersburg for three days before Lindsey had said, "Oh yeah, I forgot to tell you, Jessie Peacock called the day before yesterday to tell you Asa was in the hospital and they don't think he'll make it."

Sam had immediately left for the hospital, where he had found the Peacocks visiting with the hospital chaplain, a Methodist, who at that very moment was inviting them to participate in a heart attack support group at his church.

"That sounds nice," Asa was saying as Sam entered the room. "A fella needs spiritual support at a time like this and Lord knows my own church hasn't stepped up to the plate."

Sam sat with Asa and Jessie most of the afternoon, listening to the details of Asa's heart attack and angioplasty, wincing at all the right places, warming them up.

"I just hate that you were going through this by yourselves," Sam said. "I wish I had known. From now on, call me direct on my cell phone."

"We couldn't figure out why no one from the meeting was coming to see us," Jessie said, her chin quivering.

"Just a failure to communicate on our part," said Sam. He was using the words *failure* and *communicate* and *communication* as often as possible, not wanting to mention Lindsey's name outright, but hoping they figured it out just the same.

"It appears we have some work to do on managing our communication," he said.

After a few hours of hand-holding, Asa and Jessie had forgotten all about the Methodists and were safely returned to the welcoming bosom of Harmony Friends Meeting. Miriam and Ellis Hodge had dropped by with a casserole, the Friendly Women had sent flowers, and Dale Hinshaw had stopped by to remind them of his heart difficulties and how it had been a wake-up call, causing him to grow closer to the Lord.

Asa hadn't been thinking of the Lord. He had been thinking of his hay needing cutting. Ellis told him not to worry, that he'd round up some folks and get right on it, at which point Asa broke down and cried.

Dale, under the mistaken impression Asa was repenting, was ecstatic. "Yes, yes, just cry that sin out and let the Lord make you a new man," he said, patting Asa's hand.

Sam excused himself, and drove home in a cheerful frame of mind. Asa and Jessie were back in the fold, their hay would be mowed, and for the next hour or two Dale Hinshaw would be in another town, twenty miles away.

Ellis was as good as his word. That very afternoon he gathered a handful of farmers and began working over the Peacocks' hay field. Five tractors following one another in a staggered line, cutting hay, the dust rising about them in a swirl of grace.

3

After several years of modest growth, the attendance at Harmony Friends Meeting had leveled off. The Presbyterian church had closed its door, and ten Presbyterians had wandered in the wilderness before arriving at Harmony Friends. Sam was not all that eager to take in ten people who didn't have the gumption to keep their own church going. It was like getting ten players from a last-place team. But it looked good at the Quaker headquarters, ten new members welcomed into the meeting on one Sunday, and the superintendent had phoned Sam and asked him to give a talk on church growth at the next pastors' conference, which Sam had agreed to do.

He had been working on the speech for several months. He called it *Growth by Adoption: A New Model for Church Development.* His theory, in a nutshell, was that with mainline Christianity in decline, more churches would go broke and close. If the Quakers could hang on long enough, the displaced saints would eventually make their way to a Quaker meeting. Quakers, Sam theorized, were accustomed to living close to the bone. Economic deprivation was a weekly event. But the Methodists and Episcopalians, accustomed to large numbers and wealth, had gotten soft and folded at the first sign of trouble. You cut a Quaker meeting's budget in half, and it won't bat an eye. The Friendly Women will throw together some chicken and noodles, hold a fund-raiser, and be back in the black within a week.

The Presbyterian church sat empty for several years, until a group from Cartersburg came, looked it over, haggled a bit, then paid nineteen thousand dollars to the Presbyterians. No one knew them, so there was much speculation among the men at the Coffee Cup over what would be done with the building. Dale Hinshaw feared they were Satan worshippers and he wanted them arrested. Harvey Muldock had read, in *Reader's Digest* or *TIME*, he couldn't remember where, about old church buildings in the Midwest being bought up and used as sex clubs. It was like an exercise club, Harvey recalled. People paid fifty dollars a month for a basic membership, and thirty dollars an hour for a personal trainer.

"From what I understand," Harvey explained, "they're claiming to be a religion and the government can't touch 'em."

The men contemplated that for a moment, then Myron Farlow mentioned he'd heard a liquor store was going in there. Myron owned the Buckhorn Bar, the only tavern in town, and was clearly worried about the competition.

"Yep, I heard that, too," said Johnny Mackey. "A discount liquor store selling booze by the gallon."

Johnny Mackey, the town's mortician, had been mad at Myron Farlow ever since Myron's mother had died and he'd had her cremated and her ashes distributed over the town from an airplane. Cremated, then tossed out an airplane! A loved one burnt to a turn and pitched out a window! It made Johnny nauseous just to think of it.

As is often the case, the truth was more shocking than the rumors. The Presbyterian church had been sold to Unitarians, who painted the building inside and out, removed every symbol of the Christian faith, and within a month's time were listening to sermons about world peace, organic food, and renewable energy. They brought in folksingers from Vermont and California, had a tai chi class on Monday nights, and badgered the school board about offering a vegetarian lunch alternative for the schoolchildren.

Their pastor, a youngish man named Matt, had been a Southern Baptist minister who had read a book of liberal theology and converted to the Unitarians. He was a dazzling preacher, with a rugged jaw, a strong chin, and not an ounce of neck fat. Sam had already lost Deena Morrison and the Iverson family to the Unitarians. The Iverson twins were the only two children at Harmony Friends Meeting young enough to come down front for the children's sermon. With them gone, Sam dropped the children's sermon from the lineup, even though the elders had asked him not to.

"Yeah, well, it's not them standing up there looking like an idiot when no kids come up," he'd complained to Barbara.

Omitting the children's sermon left him with a five-minute hole to plug. He tried adding more adjectives to his sermon, repeating key sentences, and sprinkling in a few dramatic pauses, but that added less than a minute. He had once seen a television preacher speak in tongues for several minutes and wondered if that might work. He had taken a French class in college and still remembered certain phrases. (*Ou sont les toilettes les plus proches?* Where is the closest restroom? *Puis-je avoir du ketchup, s'il-vous-plaît?* Could I have ketchup with that, please?) He was reasonably certain no one else in the congregation knew

French. One Sunday, he filled the five minutes by inviting those present to stand and share their stories of spiritual renewal. Not one person spoke, not even Dale Hinshaw, who got saved once a month. It was a long, painful five minutes.

"I've been their pastor all these years and I ask them to talk about spiritual renewal and they sit there like lumps on a log. How's that supposed to make me feel?" Sam complained to his wife.

"Maybe if you had given them notice the week before, they could have come prepared to talk," she had said.

Dale had stopped by the church office the next morning to express concern about Sam's leadership. He spoke about his childhood minister, a Pastor Johnson, a great man of God. "I tell you one thing, when he got done preaching, you knew you were a sinner, that was for sure. You may have walked in thinking you were somebody, but by the time he got done with you, you knew where you stood with the Lord, and it wasn't good. I sure do miss him."

Sam had finally decided to shorten the worship five minutes, which most folks seemed to appreciate.

He was trying hard to like the Unitarian pastor, but with Matt poaching his church members right and left, it wasn't easy. Miriam and Ellis Hodge had even attended there one Sunday when their niece Amanda, away at college to study medicine, had come home for a weekend and talked them into going. Matt had given a vigorous sermon about universal health care and not one person had stood afterward to accuse him of communism. In fact, they had *applauded*! Sam had given more than seven hundred sermons at Harmony Friends and had never been applauded. Harvey Muldock had once said *Amen!* at the end of a sermon, but Sam had the sneaking suspicion he'd said it because the sermon was finally over.

Nevertheless, he invited Matt to a meeting of the ministerial association, even though Pastor Jimmy of the Harmony Worship Center had asked him not to, on account of the Unitarians not being Christian. But power has its privileges and Sam was serving as the association president that year, so had overruled him. At his first meeting, Matt had asked the other pastors for their help in organizing a parade in support of gay marriage. Right down Main Street on a Saturday morning, for all the world to see.

"Once people know the facts, they'll change their minds," Matt said. "And we ministers need to take the lead. Our congregations will respect us for it."

The other pastors believed Matt was overly optimistic, if not outright delusional. Nevertheless, Sam was sympathetic to the cause, if only because Dale Hinshaw would be against it. A gay rights parade in Harmony, led by the ministers. He thought of attending, then decided against, suspecting it would be his last act as the minister of Harmony Friends Meeting, that not even Miriam Hodge could save his job.

Sam had thanked Matt for his suggestion, then suggested they give it a little more thought, maybe another year or two, or even five. Sam was hoping to keep his job long enough to get his sons through college.

Matt held the parade anyway, leading ten Unitarians up and down the sidewalk in front of the *Harmony Herald* office until Bob Miles came out and took their picture for that week's paper. Dale Hinshaw was there, carrying a sign that read on one side, "All have sinned and fallen short of the glory of God," and advertised the church's chicken noodle dinner on the other. "Come enjoy homemade chicken and noodles, pies, and cakes!! All you can eat for $7.50, tea or lemonade included!"

The *Herald* was swamped with letters to the editor, running three to one against the Unitarians. Predictions of their eternal damnation were made, along with several invitations to leave town. Pastor Jimmy at the Harmony Worship Center launched a ten-week sermon series on biblical marriage, culminating in a visit from an evangelist who had been gay before getting right with the Lord and becoming a heterosexual. Bob Miles was elated. It had been years since any single picture had generated such excitement, not since Nora Nagle had portrayed the Virgin Mary in the annual Christmas pageant wearing nothing but a bathrobe.

Sam lay low, working on his church growth speech, avoiding his office so as not to get roped into conversation. But Barbara was tired of holding her tongue and wrote to the *Herald*, applauding the Unitarians and welcoming them to town. It infuriated Fern Hampton, who called for Barbara's expulsion from the Friendly Women's Circle. Sam's mother, Gloria, was mortified. Her own daughter-in-law exiled, banished from the Circle. Providentially, Miriam Hodge called for a committee to be formed to examine the matter, thereby ensuring nothing would happen.

Three women of the Circle left to join the Harmony Worship Center, and the Unitarian church gained five new members, Democrats from Cartersburg. Thankfully, it was autumn, the Corn and Sausage Days Festival was fast approaching, as was the Chicken Noodle Dinner, and passions cooled with the shortening days.

4

The weekend of the Corn and Sausage Days dawned story-book perfect, which is how almost every disastrous day begins. The heat of summer had broken, and Saturday morning was crisp and clear. By noon it was sixty degrees, a new Sausage Queen had been crowned, and the women of the Circle had served 532 dinners, a new record, with another fifty people in line, stretching out the meetinghouse doors and down the front steps. Shaken by the departure of Deena Morrison and the Iversons to the Unitarians, Sam was working the crowd, greeting people, inviting them to return the next day for worship and leftover noodles.

By two thirty, everyone had been fed, and the kitchen cleanup was well under way. Sam was in his office putting the finishing touches on his sermon when the church telephone rang. It was Pastor Matt from the Unitarian church, waylaid by the flu, vomiting on the hour and half hour.

"I have a wedding to do at three thirty, and I'm in no shape to do it. Can you cover for me, Sam? I'll owe you one."

Sam glanced at his watch, and feeling charitable said, "Happy to help. Who's the happy couple."

"Chris Marshall and Kelly Johnson. Nice folks. You'll like 'em. First marriage for both of them."

"Hmm," Sam said. "Don't know them. Where are they from?"

"Cartersburg," Matt said. "They were one of our first couples here. They've been dating about four years, but living together for a year or so. Does that bother you?"

"Well, the way I see it, if the church thinks it's a sin for an unmarried couple to live together, why should I object when they want to get married," Sam said. "Seems to me they're trying to set matters right." Sam paused. "The only thing is, I've never done a Unitarian wedding. Can I use the Quaker vows?"

"Unitarians often write their own vows," Matt said. "I've sat down with the couple and gone through the service. You just need to stand up front, listen to the vows, and say a prayer of blessing at the end."

"I can do that," Sam said.

"It's pretty straightforward," Matt added. "No attendants. The couple, Chris and Kelly, will come down the aisle together, there'll be a few readings, then the couple will give their vows."

"Piece of cake," Sam said.

Matt thanked Sam profusely, then Sam hurried home, showered, changed into his suit, and was at the Unitarian church with five minutes to spare.

The church was full, the pews crowded, a smattering of latecomers clustered in the back, searching for an empty seat. Deena Morrison and Judy Iverson were there, looking treasonous. Bob Miles from the *Herald* was standing in the doorway. He glanced up as Sam entered the narthex.

"Fancy seeing you here," Bob said.

"Matt's sick," Sam explained. "He phoned to see if I could help out."

"Awful nice of you," Bob said. "And brave, too. Not just any pastor would do this."

"Oh, most of us would. We pitch in and help each other out," Sam said modestly. "We wouldn't want to leave a couple in the lurch."

Sam wondered why performing a wedding required bravery. He'd never known a pastor to be injured at a wedding, after all.

The pianist began, Sam slipped discreetly along the side of the sanctuary, taking his place at the front, facing the congregation.

The couple appeared at the back of the church, stepping forward slowly to the tune of the wedding march.

They stopped before Sam, smiling.

A young man came forward and read from the thirteenth chapter of First Corinthians about noisy gongs and clanging cymbals and the power of love. Then a man with a ponytail read from Kahlil Gibran's book *The Prophet*, about there being spaces in your togetherness and moving seas between the shores of your souls and not eating from the same loaf of bread. Sam didn't understand much of it, but he smiled anyway and nodded his head in all the right places.

The man with the ponytail sat down, and Sam turned to face the couple, Chris and Kelly, taking them both in for the first time. Chris was finely featured, with shoulder-length blond hair, and was dressed in a simple, lovely gown. Kelly had short, spiky hair, neatly gelled, and was attired in black pants and a tailored jacket. Not a suit, actually, Sam thought, more like a pantsuit. And pearls. Which is when it occurred to Sam he was inadvertently performing his first same-gender wedding.

He paused, wishing more parents gave their children names like Ralph, Betty, Elmer, and Hazel. Good, old-fashioned, straightforward names. Whatever happened to those names? Now people named their children Drew, Pat, Jordan, Riley, Shawn, and Morgan. What kind of names were those? *Names that confused people and got ministers in trouble*, Sam thought. *Chris and Kelly? How was he to know which gender they were? For Pete's sake!*

This was Sam's ninety-second wedding, which meant he had mastered the pause. He stopped for a moment as if he were considering the solemnity of the occasion, desperately thinking how best to proceed. Chris and Kelly looked at him expectantly, then at one another, their faces radiating happiness. On top of his chest of drawers, there was a picture of him and Barbara on their wedding day, smiling. Sam called it his I-can't-believe-you've-agreed-to-marry-me smile. It was that same exact smile.

Bob Miles was making his way toward the front of the church, snapping pictures as he drew nearer to the couple. Sam could just imagine the headline. *Quaker Pastor Sam Gardner Performs Town's First Gay Marriage!* He wished Matt would hurry up and get better so he could kill him.

Sam leaned toward Chris and Kelly and said, "Can we go somewhere a bit more private? We need to talk."

He turned to the congregation. "We'll be right back. Don't leave."

He guided them to a small room, where they sat down. He said, "I wasn't aware this was a same-gender wedding. They're not legal in our state, you know."

"We know," Chris said. "We went to the county clerk's office to get a license, but she wouldn't issue us one. We've decided not to wait for the state to validate our relationship."

"But I'm not supposed to do them," Sam said. "The superintendent of our yearly meeting told me specifically, 'Sam, don't marry gay people.'"

The year before, Sam had accidentally married a man secretly married to two other women. The newspaper in the city had learned of it and written an article on bigamy. They had scrounged up a copy of the marriage license with Sam's signature on it and published it in the paper. The next day, the Quaker superintendent had talked with Sam about whom he could and couldn't marry. He'd reminded him several times not to marry gay couples, people who were already married, or minors.

"I thought Quakers believed in equality," Kelly said. "Why won't you marry gays and lesbians?"

"The Quakers in these parts are more conservative," Sam said. "I would get in a lot of trouble if I married you. My superintendent told me, very specifically, that I couldn't marry gay people. I'd probably lose my job."

"Even if it weren't a Quaker wedding?" Kelly asked.

"What do you mean?"

"I mean we're in a Unitarian church, in front of a Unitarian congregation," Kelly explained. "We've written our own vows. And since we don't have a marriage license, you don't have to sign anything. All you're doing is listening to us make our vows, then offering a prayer. Surely your superintendent can't forbid you from praying."

Sam thought for a moment. "I wouldn't think so," he said.

"Then what's the harm?" Chris asked.

"I guess when you look at it that way, there'd be no harm in my saying a prayer. I'm sure the Quakers won't mind that."

Even though Sam was a seasoned pastor, his naïveté could be breathtaking.

They returned to the sanctuary, where Sam thanked everyone for their patience. Chris and Kelly recited their vows from memory, while Sam looked on, then caught himself just in time before pronouncing them husband and wife. He launched into prayer, thanking God for letting them live in a free country and for the food that nourished their bodies. He had never been good at extemporaneous prayer and usually wound up thanking God for various things, none of them relevant to the event at hand.

Everyone present applauded, Bob Miles snapped a few more pictures, Chris and Kelly walked down the aisle hand in hand, then everyone went down to the basement and snacked on peanuts and mints and drank punch made from ice cream and 7-Up.

Sam was standing near the punch bowl when Bob Miles approached him. "Like I said, it sure was nice of you to do this. Not many pastors around here would conduct a lesbian marriage. They'd be afraid of getting fired."

"It's not like I married them," Sam pointed out. "I didn't sign a license or anything. Just said a prayer. I don't see how I can get in trouble for that."

Deena Morrison poured herself a glass of punch, then made her way over to Sam. She was in tears. "That's the loveliest wedding I've ever seen. I'm so happy for them. And I'm proud of you, Sam. This will upset a lot of people, but you did it anyway."

"Oh, I don't think people will be all that upset," said Sam. "I really didn't do anything."

"Don't diminish your bravery, Sam. What you did was beautiful and courageous and I'm proud of you," Deena said. "It makes me want to come back to meeting."

"We sure have missed you," Sam said. "It would be wonderful if you returned."

"The Unitarians are nice, but it just isn't the same."

Sam was elated to learn of her unhappiness.

He stayed another half hour, then walked home, pleased as punch. What a day it had been! A new Sausage Queen, record noodle sales, a lovely wedding skillfully conducted to keep him out of trouble, and Deena Morrison on the verge of returning to Harmony Friends Meeting. Climbing the steps to his front porch, he danced a little jig, confident things were finally turning his way.

5

Barbara Gardner was tired of Harmony, tired of certain people telling her what she could and couldn't think, tired of picking up after her husband and sons, and tired most of all of being asked to do the worst jobs in the meeting just because she was married to the pastor. Truth be told, she was a bit tired of the pastor, too.

The week before, she and Sam had had a big fight, their worst ever. She had locked him out of the bedroom and he'd slept on the couch. With Levi gone, and Addison pulling at the traces to leave, she had mentioned looking for a job.

"I have a perfectly fine degree in library science I've never used," she told Sam. "I'm tired of being short of money. The library is looking for an assistant librarian. I'm going to apply."

"Will you be gone evenings?" Sam asked.

"I'm sure I'll work some of them."

"Who'll cook our supper?" Sam had asked.

She was going to slug him, but stopped herself just in time and locked him out of the bedroom instead. He had stood outside their bedroom door for ten minutes, sniveling, then had gone down to the kitchen and had a bowl of Cocoa Puffs for supper.

"Who'll cook our supper. He actually said, 'Who'll cook our supper,'" Barbara complained to her mother the next day. "It was all I could do not to throttle him."

"That's a man for you. Your father's the same way. I spent two hours fixing supper last night and he told me the pot roast was tough. Can you believe that?"

She went on and on, describing in great detail the many faults of Barbara's father. Barbara remembered why she seldom phoned her mother.

"Mom, can I talk to you for five minutes without you complaining about Dad? I'm dying here. If something doesn't change, I'm going to kill Sam or have an affair."

"Kill him," Barbara's mother advised. "Get a jury of women and you'll walk. But wait until Addison leaves for college. You don't want him to find the body."

"Oh, yes, about that. Our number-two son wants to join the army."

"Oh my Lord. What is he thinking? Why does he want to do that?"

"He told us he wanted an adventure. That he didn't want to be like Sam and end up spending most of his life in the same place. Plus, think about it. He was just a kid when 9/11 happened and all he's heard is how the soldiers are heroes. What young man wouldn't want to be a hero?"

"I suppose you're right, but I can't bear the thought of him being in a war."

"We can't, either, but his mind is made up."

They kvetched about men and boys and how sometimes they were indistinguishable, and when they finished talking,

Barbara had decided not to kill Sam or have an affair. But she did walk the three blocks to the library to fill out an application, then drove to Cartersburg and bought a laptop computer so she wouldn't have to keep asking Sam's permission to use his computer.

She'd been asking for one for a year and he'd always said, "Let's wait until the next paycheck. Money's a little tight now."

"Yeah," she wanted to say. "Of course it's tight when you go to college and seminary for eight years, then come back to your hometown to a job that pays chicken feed, but you put up with it because you're nostalgic and don't want to live anywhere you haven't spent your entire life."

She wanted to say that, but she didn't.

Moving to Harmony had been Sam's dream, not hers. She had gone along with it for the sake of their sons. It was a good place to raise children, but not such a good place for adults who valued independent thought. After she'd written a letter to the editor welcoming the Unitarians to town, Dale Hinshaw had fired off a letter to the *Herald* taking her to task. Bob Miles had printed it, like the muckraker he was, and Sam had done nothing about it.

"It's a free country, what do you want me to do?" he'd asked her.

"You could stand up to Dale Hinshaw for once," she'd said. "Just once, you could go up to him and say, 'Dale, if you want to pick on me, that's one thing, but leave my wife out of it.'"

"I could lose my job doing that."

"Fine, I'll talk with him," Barbara said. "I have a few things I've been wanting to say to him and it's about time I did."

"Don't do that. I could lose my job."

"Yeah, well, you could lose your wife, too. Have you ever thought of that?"

She would never leave him, but he didn't need to know that. It was good to let him think it was a possibility. She'd taken to introducing him as her first husband, just to keep him on his toes.

As for Sam losing his job, it was nearly impossible to get an entire group of Quakers to agree on anything, though they could occasionally rally and kick a pastor to the curb, if need be. So Sam lived in constant fear they might unite around one great cause and he would be out on his keister, a fear he regularly shared with Barbara, to her deep aggravation.

He'd taken her out to dinner to soften her up, to the seafood buffet at the Holiday Inn in Cartersburg, as if two pieces of greasy fish and a few rubbery scallops were adequate compensation for not defending his wife. When they got home, she went straight to bed with a stomachache. He'd come into the bedroom looking for *that. That* was something she still enjoyed, but not with a gut full of nasty fish congealing in her intestines. He was in the bullpen, warming up, ready to step up to the plate, when the check valve blew. She barely made it to the bathroom. He'd slept on the couch that night, too.

6

The Monday morning after the wedding, Sam woke up early and went for a walk out in the country toward Ellis and Miriam Hodge's farm. He arrived at their house just as they were pulling out of their driveway. Ellis rolled to a stop and lowered his window.

"Howdy, Sam. Out for a walk I see."

"You bet. What are the Hodges up to this beautiful morning?"

"Don't you remember, Sam?" Miriam said. "We're going to the Smoky Mountains."

In all the years of their marriage, Ellis and Miriam had never flown anywhere, and gave considerable thought before driving beyond the county line. Ellis didn't trust engines. He believed all engines were as persnickety as the engine on his Farmall tractor and he'd have to climb out on the wing, thirty thousand feet in the air, and whack it with a hammer or duct tape a fuel line to keep it running. Distrusting the internal combustion engine, he seldom drove beyond walking distance from home, which gave him about a five-mile radius. But now he was throwing caution to the wind and driving four hundred miles to the Smoky Mountains. The month before he had noticed blood on his toothbrush and had convinced himself he was dying of cancer, so he was going to the Smoky Mountains, which he'd always wanted to see before he died.

"How long will you be gone?" Sam asked.

"Should be back next Sunday," Ellis said. "Unless we have trouble with the truck, then there's no telling." He looked anxious, thinking about blown engines, flat tires, and fuel explosions.

"Traveling mercies," Sam said. "Enjoy yourselves."

It was a half-hour walk back into town, past the town garage, down Main Street to the meetinghouse. Technically, Monday was Sam's day off, but he went in just the same and found Lindsey Hinshaw in the office, reading the church's mail.

"Good morning, Lindsey," he said.

"I thought today was your day off," she said.

"It is. I just wanted to stop by and check on things. Any messages on the answering machine."

"Pastor Matt called to thank you for helping him out this past Saturday. The superintendent called and wants you to call him back as soon as you can. And my grandpa called. He and Fern Hampton have called a special meeting of the elders tonight at seven p.m. and want you there."

"Criminetly," Sam said. "It's my day off. I don't want to go to a meeting tonight. Would you please call him back and tell him I'm not available."

"He won't like that."

"This happens every week. I take a day off and someone calls me with something that just can't wait."

He left the meetinghouse in a sour mood, his formerly pleasant day thoroughly ruined. Barbara was in the basement doing the laundry when he got home. "Dale Hinshaw phoned," she yelled up the stairs. "There's a meeting tonight at seven. He wants you there. I told him it was your day off, but he said it was an emergency."

"Everything is an emergency," Sam muttered. "Do this, do that, be here, be there. Hurry up. I need it now. You'd think the world was ending."

He yelled down the stairs to Barbara, "If he thinks I'm just going to drop everything because he asked me to, he's got another think coming."

Sam arrived at the meeting five minutes late to show Dale and Fern he couldn't be pushed around.

Dale Hinshaw, Fern Hampton, Bea Majors, and her sister, Opal, were in the meetinghouse basement, seated around a folding table, waiting for Sam to arrive. Miriam Hodge was the other member of the elders' committee, the only one with a functioning brain. It mystified Sam that in a congregation of reasonably bright folks, four of the dimmest people served as elders. If it weren't for Miriam Hodge, the elders' committee would have steered the church off the cliff years ago.

Sam greeted them, then turned to Dale and said, "So what's the emergency?"

"With Miriam gone, we'll need an acting clerk," Dale said, ignoring Sam's question. "Any suggestions?"

"I think you should be in charge, Dale," Fern said. Bea and Opal Majors nodded their agreement.

"I thought only the clerk could call a meeting," Sam said.

"Well, Miriam can't very well call a meeting if she's not in town, now can she?" Dale said.

"And you're sure this can't wait?" Sam asked.

"Not one more minute," Dale said.

Sam hated it when Miriam missed a meeting.

"Okay, what's so important it can't wait until Miriam gets back?" Sam asked.

"I got a call from the superintendent this morning and he's awful upset," Dale said. "Have you talked to him yet, Sam?"

Sam had forgotten to return his phone call. "No, not lately. What did he want now?"

"He told me you married two women this past Saturday," Dale said. "In direct violation of our beliefs."

"I don't think it's accurate to speak of 'our beliefs' since we all don't believe the same thing," Sam said.

"Were you or were you not there?" Fern said.

"Yes, I was there," Sam said. "I said a prayer of blessing. Pastor Matt at the Unitarian church was sick, so I stepped in at the last minute to help."

"That's it, you're fired," Fern snapped.

"Opal and I have a nephew who would make a fine minister," Bea suggested. "Should we call him?"

"We've been through this before," Sam said. "You can't just fire me. That has to be decided by the congregation."

This was the third time Dale and Fern had tried to fire Sam. Once for not wearing a suit and tie at Easter, and another time for suggesting they cancel the Chicken Noodle Dinner. Fern had spent an entire elders' meeting complaining that none of the younger people wanted to help with the dinner and she was tired of doing all the work and if people didn't want to work, then maybe they should just cancel the dinner, which Sam said was fine with him, that he was tired of it, too. Then Fern said it was a shame when the church's pastor lost his passion for ministry and that Sam should quit so they could get themselves a minister with a heart for the Lord.

"The superintendent said he's going to have to fire you," Dale said.

"Yeah, well, he can't fire me, either," Sam said. At least, he didn't think so, but maybe the rules had changed.

Their superintendent routinely confused himself with God and had gotten in the habit of handing down edicts to the pastors, most of which Sam ignored, since the superintendent lived two hours away and hadn't darkened the door of Harmony Friends Meeting in three years.

Bea Majors chimed in. "I don't see how you can remain our pastor after this. The congregation won't stand for it."

She had him there. With Miriam Hodge gone, and Asa Peacock out of commission with a bad heart, Sam was hanging on by a thread.

He sat quietly, fuming. Fern Hampton and the Major sisters had never been married. Dale Hinshaw had reduced his wife to a mindless robot. Now they wanted to fire him for praying for two people who genuinely cared for one another. He couldn't believe he'd given up his one free evening for this.

"Well, folks, it's my day off, so I'm going home," Sam said.

"We're not done here," Dale said, his voice rising. "What are we going to tell the superintendent?"

"Tell him to mind his own business," Sam suggested. "Or tell him to grow up. Or maybe you should tell him people won't always do what he wants and he'd better get used to the idea. Take your pick, Dale."

He walked by Grant's Hardware store on the way home. He sometimes envied Uly Grant his vocation. Why couldn't his father have owned a hardware store? Hardware stores sold nuts and bolts to anyone, straight or gay, black or white, male or female, Catholic or Protestant, Democrat or Republican; it didn't matter. Sam had known Uly Grant since the first grade. They'd sat together for twelve years, in alphabetical order, and he'd not once known Uly Grant to be mad at anything or anyone. Sam thought there was something about hardware stores that made a man content.

Uly was locking the front door of the store as Sam went past. He fell into step beside Sam.

"Well, hello, Sam Gardner. How the heck are you?"

"Good enough, I suppose. How are the Grants?"

"We're doing fine," Uly said. "Hey, I heard you might be leaving us."

"Who told you that?" Sam asked.

"Lindsey Hinshaw mentioned something about it."

"Well, she was mistaken," said Sam.

"I hope you don't, Sam. I just thought maybe you'd found a church that could pay a little more. Couldn't hardly blame you, what with your boys heading off to college."

"Barbara's interviewing for a job at the library. That'll help."

"Not that I want you to move, but if you ever do, be sure to let me know. We might be interested in buying your house. Always liked that house."

"Don't start packing your things just yet," Sam said. "We're staying put."

Sam walked on, thinking about Lindsey Hinshaw, wishing Frank, his previous secretary, hadn't moved to North Carolina. Frank had kept the malcontents in line. He had been in the military and understood warfare. Sam suspected Lindsey was a spy, sent by Dale to infiltrate the pastor's office and sabotage Sam's best efforts. She'd bear watching, that one.

7

Barbara woke early the next morning for her interview at the library. She'd had her hair styled the day before, had bought a new outfit at the JCPenney in Cartersburg, and had purchased a teeth-whitening kit at the Rexall, but had fallen asleep with the whitening strips on. When she smiled, she looked like a car with its brights on. She made a mental note not to smile.

She was counting on this job. Sam was losing interest in his ministry at Harmony. She could tell. The first ten years, he'd been excited, full of ideas, gabbing about his job. Now he just complained. They needed a plan B, something to fall back on, and her getting a job was probably it. She wished Miss Rudy were still the librarian. She'd be sure to get the job. But Miss Rudy had retired that summer after sixty years at the helm, navigating the library through the choppy waters of budget cuts from town board members who hadn't read a book since high school. Then the library board voted to bring in DVDs, and that had been the final straw. Movies in the library! All manner of sex and violence and foul language. The first box of movies had arrived on a Monday morning and by noon that same day Miss Rudy had written her letter of resignation and put her house up for sale. Two weeks later she moved to the city to live with her cousin.

The new librarian, a Ms. Woodrum, was fresh out of college and referred to herself as a media specialist. She'd removed Miss Rudy's NO TALKING PERMITTED sign, and brought in bean bag chairs for the children to flop down on like fat slugs. For the first time in living memory, a child could enter the library and be reasonably confident he would leave alive. Then Ms. Woodrum had opened the library on Sundays, in direct defiance of Scripture, or so said Pastor Jimmy of the Harmony Worship Center, who wasn't quite sure where the verse was, but knew it was in there somewhere. Then, without consulting anyone, she had ordered a book on sex education, causing much wailing and gnashing of teeth, all of which she ignored.

Barbara arrived an hour early for the interview and read *National Geographic*, which Miss Rudy hadn't carried on account of the pictures of naked African women. A few minutes before the interview, the new librarian walked past the periodicals, saw Barbara, introduced herself, shook her hand, and ushered her into her office.

"Thank you for this interview, Ms. Woodrum," Barbara said. "I'm very grateful for this opportunity."

"Drop the Ms. Woodrum. I'm Janet," she said. And though they had never met, Barbara felt immediately at ease. After a wide-ranging conversation in which they discussed books and college and teeth whiteners, Janet offered her the job, then asked, "Oh, one more thing. I know your husband is a minister, but can you work the occasional Sunday?"

Barbara thought about Dale Hinshaw discussing the seven-headed beast of Revelation in Sunday school, realized she'd finally found a way to escape, and said she would be happy to work on Sunday, or any other day.

"Great! When can you start?"

"Right now," said Barbara.

"Let's get going then. I'd like you to shadow me this first week, learn the ropes, then we'll turn you loose on the place."

It was a splendid day for Barbara. Working in a library, surrounded by books, discussing important ideas with intelligent people. The library closed at 8 p.m., but she and Janet stayed over, shelving the last of the books that had been returned that day. She walked home, tired but happy, pleased to be doing something other than housework.

Sam and Addison were watching television and eating bacon, wiping their greasy fingers on their pants.

"Bacon? Is that all you're having?" Barbara asked.

"It wasn't just bacon," Sam said. "It was bacon-wrapped bacon."

"Yeah, it was my idea," said Addison. "We deep-fried it."

The stove was splattered with bacon grease, which Barbara ignored, though not without difficulty. What was it with men? She prepared herself a salad. Sam wandered into the kitchen.

He leaned against the counter. "So how was your day?"

She smiled. "You are now looking at the assistant librarian of the Harmony Public Library."

Sam laughed. "Well, look at you." He hugged her, then arched his eyebrows. "Did I ever tell you I have a thing for librarians?"

"I wouldn't put it past you."

"Hey, now you'll know who's checking out the sex education book," Sam said.

"First thing I looked up," she said. "And you would be amazed. Wish I could tell you their names, but I can't."

"Tell me their initials."

"I can't."

"Just the first letter of their first name," he pleaded. "And if I guess, just nod your head."

"Can't do it. It's privileged information."

"Do I know him?" Sam asked.

"How do you know it's a him?"

" 'Cause hers don't check out sex education books."

"Oh, you have a lot to learn, Sam Gardner."

"Just tell me who it was."

"Nope, can't say. But I will tell you this: You would be shocked. You wouldn't guess who in a million years."

"Are they members of the meeting?"

"Maybe, maybe not. I can't say."

"If they're members of the meeting, I really should know," Sam said.

"Why is that any of your business?"

"Just tell me," Sam begged.

No one loved a secret more than Sam Gardner. He became a pastor to learn people's secrets. He knew things about people in Harmony that would curl the hair. And he always told Barbara. Always. Not that she'd ever asked, but once he knew a secret he had to tell someone. Secrets leaked out of him, like air from a punctured tire, like pus from a wound. If he had been a spy and had ever been captured, he would have spilled the beans in five minutes for a glass of water.

It had been a long day and Barbara was tired. She went to bed early, not giving Sam the opportunity to prove his attraction to librarians in the manner he desired. Instead, he cleaned the kitchen, picked up the downstairs, and folded the laundry, there being a myriad of ways to show affection and appreciation.

8

S am was seated at his desk the next morning when he heard
Lindsey say, "Hi, Grandpa. What are you doing here?"

As if she didn't know, Sam thought.

"This is my granddaughter, Lindsey," he heard Dale say.
"She's the Director of Communications here at the meeting."

"A pleasure to meet you," an unctuous voice, dripping with
insincerity, responded. "God bless you for your ministry here."

The Quaker superintendent! Sam wanted to hide under his
desk, and would have if Lindsey hadn't said, "Yes, he's here. Go
right on in."

When Sam had become a pastor, the superintendent at the
time had been a calm, caring man, a pastor to the pastors, with
a genuine love for people, and prone to err on the side of grace.
But he had retired, and had been followed by a string of short-
termers, coasting toward retirement. The latest superintendent
had come along with a plan to start new meetings and double
membership, which hadn't yet happened, though he had managed to run off several good pastors whose theology wasn't to

his liking. He was a strutter, a man given to arm-waving and self-righteousness, two qualities Sam had never admired in clergy. Now here he was, standing in the office doorway, blocking Sam's retreat.

"Sam, my child, so good to see you."

He was a year younger than Sam, but referred to all the pastors as his children, no matter their age. Except for the women ministers, whom he called his girls. He was as good an argument against institutional religion as Sam had ever met.

All his life, Sam had strived mightily to make everyone happy, but since crossing the half-century mark he had decided to let others make him happy for a change, and figured Dale and the superintendent were a good place to start.

"Well, look what the cat drug in," Sam said. "Come in, gents. Sit down, take a load off. I'd offer you something to drink, but we're out of everything."

They sat down. Lindsey followed them in, standing in the doorway.

"What can I do for you?" Sam asked.

"I'll not beat around the bush," the superintendent said. "I heard you conducted a gay wedding."

"Not exactly," Sam said. "I offered a prayer at the wedding of two women."

"It wasn't a wedding, since homosexuals can't marry," Dale said.

"Well, if it wasn't a wedding, then I guess your visit was pointless," Sam said, smiling at the superintendent. "Sorry you had to drive all that way for nothing."

"Whether or not it was a wedding isn't the point. Your very presence implies acceptance of what happened," the superintendent said. "And not just your acceptance, but the acceptance of this congregation, and by virtue of that, the acceptance of our entire yearly meeting."

"I was invited to offer a prayer for two young women and I did so. I saw nothing wrong with praying for two people wanting to share their lives with one another."

"The Lord condemns it," Dale snapped.

"That's your opinion," Sam said. "Not mine."

Lindsey spoke from the doorway. "Come on, Grandpa, leave Sam alone."

This was certainly a surprise.

"This doesn't concern you, Lindsey," Dale blustered. "Go back to your desk."

"Dale, I'll thank you not to order my staff around," Sam said. "Lindsey, this is your church, too. You can say what you wish."

Dale stared at Sam like a landed fish walloped by a two-by-four, his mouth agape. "I knew you would turn her against me."

"Don't be silly, Grandpa. I'm not against you. I just don't agree with you."

"Let's get back to the matter at hand," the superintendent said. "I can't have my pastors running around condoning this sort of thing."

"I am not *your* pastor," Sam informed him. "I'm my own man. You don't own me."

"According to the Oversight Committee, pastors report to me."

"Ah, yes, the Oversight Committee," Sam said. "The committee you formed without asking the rest of us. They have no authority over me. God has called me to ministry, and this congregation invited me here. Until God tells me I can't pray for people, I will continue to do so."

"We'll see about that," Dale said.

"Indeed we will," Sam said. He turned to face the superintendent. "The church has plenty of small-minded people afraid of change. Our leaders need to move us beyond that, not encourage it."

For someone who wasn't good on his feet, Sam was surprised by his burst of eloquence and wished it were being recorded.

The superintendent rose to his feet. "Given the circumstances, I'll have to retract my offer for you to speak at our next pastors' conference. It's clear to me you are no longer in the Spirit. In fact, I prefer you not attend at all."

Sam had never liked attending pastors' retreats, but now that he knew the superintendent didn't want him there, he'd be sure to go. If he were still around, that is.

"Gentlemen, I have work to do. I trust you can find the door."

"This matter is not over," the superintendent said.

"No, I suppose it isn't," Sam said. "But this conversation is. I have other things to do. Next time, please make an appointment."

The superintendent strode from the office with Dale in tow.

"I'll be gone within the month," he told Lindsey after they had left. "You watch and see."

"I love my grandpa, but he's wrong," Lindsey said. "And I'm going to talk to him and tell him so."

"Lindsey, I appreciate your support, but don't stick your neck out for me. I don't want there to be hard feelings in your family."

"He's the one who was all hot for me to take this job," she said. "He's probably regretting that now."

Even though it was only Wednesday, Sam went to work on his sermon. It was a scorcher of a message, in which he quoted Jesus and the prophets of old, going hammer and tongs against injustice and narrow-mindedness. If the elders didn't like it, they could always attend the Harmony Worship Center, where they sang one-line songs projected on big screens and couldn't make a noodle to save their souls.

9

The same morning Sam Gardner was set upon by Dale and the superintendent, Miriam and Ellis Hodge were in Gatlinburg, Tennessee, strolling from one souvenir shop to another.

"I wouldn't give you a plug nickel for this junk," Ellis grumbled. "I can't believe we drove four hundred miles to see this."

Miriam didn't point out that the vacation had been his idea.

"Let's drive over into North Carolina," Miriam suggested. "We could go to Asheville and see the Biltmore Estate."

"Better not. I think something's wrong with the truck. We probably ought to head home."

It had been like this since the second morning of their trip, when they'd had a flat tire.

"It's an omen," he'd said. "I think we should go back. I think the house is on fire."

They'd phoned his brother Ralph, who'd told them their house was fine, but that Sam was in trouble for marrying two lesbians.

"He did what?" Ellis had asked.

"Married two women at the Unitarian church. Least that's what Asa Peacock told me. Dale and Fern are all worked up about it and trying to get him fired."

"Well, that's nothing new," Ellis had said. "They've been trying to get him fired ever since we hired him. Anything else going on?"

"Nope, that's about it."

"You sure our house isn't burning?" Ellis had asked hopefully, desperate to return home.

"I'm looking out the window at it right now. Everything's fine."

They had arrived in Gatlinburg and checked into a honeymoon hotel, sleeping in a heart-shaped bed that sagged in the middle. They slept on top of the blankets with their clothes on, staring at themselves in the mirror above the bed, somewhat embarrassed, praying they wouldn't run into someone they knew.

Gatlinburg was a disappointment, a haphazard pile of shops selling souvenirs made in China. More than once, they were squeezed off the sidewalk to let groups of hefty people pass.

"I've never seen so many obese people gathered in one place in my entire life," Ellis grumbled. "It's like a convention of fat people."

"Be nice," Miriam said.

"And to think they cut down trees to make this place."

Ellis had become more opinionated as he had aged, a development Miriam found most distressing. She worried he was losing his mind. On several occasions she had caught him in the barn listening to fanatics on the radio rant about the government. It was depressing the cows, causing their milk output to drop, so she had taken her hedge clippers and cut the radio's electrical cord.

They were at the hotel when Miriam's cell phone rang. It was Fern Hampton, who made small talk about the weather, then asked when they might be back.

"Probably late Sunday," Miriam said. "Why? Is there a problem?"

"Oh, no, everything's fine. Just wanted to make sure you were all right. You and Ellis enjoy yourselves and don't worry about a thing. Good-bye for now."

"That woman is up to no good," Miriam said. "She's never cared whether we were all right. She's up to something. Mark my words."

"Maybe we should go home," Ellis said.

"Maybe we should," Miriam agreed.

But they didn't go immediately. Instead, they drove into the park, which was beautiful, and shared a picnic beside a stream, and watched trout swimming in a deep pool underneath a log, then stretched out for a nap on the mossy bank. For one pleasant afternoon, Ellis was grateful for their vacation and understood why others might occasionally wish to leave home for lovely moments such as these.

10

That same afternoon, Dale Hinshaw, Fern Hampton, and Bea and Opal Majors were seated around Fern's kitchen table, plotting Sam's overthrow.

"It's got to happen this Sunday, before Miriam and Ellis get home," Fern said. "They're always sticking up for Sam."

"He's got to go," Dale said. "But there are folks who like him. I think even Lindsey likes him." He shook his head, mystified. "I don't know what's gotten into that girl."

"She and Sam sure have gotten close lately," Bea said. "I wouldn't be surprised if something's going on there. You know how ministers are with their secretaries."

"Lindsey's not that kind of girl," Dale said. "She wouldn't do that."

"You didn't think she'd support sodomites," Fern snapped. "Maybe she's not the little angel you think she is."

"She might have to go, too," Opal said. "Especially if she and Sam are sleeping around."

"You know they are," Bea said. "Why else would she stick up for him?"

"I don't know what Barbara sees in that man," Fern said. "She's working at the library now, you know. Probably realized their marriage was falling apart and she needed a job. I've seen it happen time and again. Maybe it's time someone told her what he's up to. What a sad marriage it must be."

It was ironic that Fern Hampton, who had never been able to convince even one man his life would be better with her, would consider herself an expert on marriage.

"He's been cozying up to the Unitarians. I think if folks knew that, he'd be out of here," Dale said. "We ought to send out an e-mail and call for a meeting of the church."

"Can we do that?" Fern said.

"Sure we can. We're the elders, after all," Dale said. "I have a list of everyone's e-mail addresses that Lindsey put together."

Dale's missive went out that very night, a long diatribe, sprinkled with Scripture verses, detailing Sam's various short-comings, chief among them his utter disregard for tradition and authority and the Lord. Dale observed that Sam had recently been seen in the company of Unitarians, who everyone knew didn't believe in God and were going straight to hell.

Sam's mother, Gloria Gardner, phoned Sam the minute she read the e-mail. "What do you mean, you don't believe in God? When did that happen?"

"What are you talking about?"

"I just got an e-mail from Dale saying you don't believe in God."

Sam assured his mother he still believed in God.

"He also said you conducted a same-gender marriage," his mother said.

"It was an accident," Sam said. "I didn't realize it was two women. And I didn't conduct the wedding, at least not officially. All I did was say a prayer."

"Well, there's nothing wrong with that. We're supposed to pray for people."

"That's what I thought," Sam said.

"What are you going to do, honey?" his mom asked.

"I'm going to go to bed," Sam said.

"No, I mean about the e-mail."

Sam fell silent for a moment, thinking. "I tell you, Mom. I'm tired of this nonsense. If the meeting wants to fire me for praying for two women, so be it. I'm not sure I want to even pastor a meeting where that would be an issue."

"Oh, no, don't say that. We need you."

"That's a matter of opinion. Dale and the superintendent came to see me this morning. They obviously think the church would get along fine without me."

"Oh, Dale is just an old sourpuss. Ignore him."

"He's pretty hard to ignore," Sam said.

"I'm going to call him and give him a piece of my mind," Gloria said.

"Don't, Mom. That'll just make things worse."

"Somebody needs to rein him in. What about Miriam? Where is she in all of this?"

"She and Ellis are on vacation," Sam said. "Won't be back until Sunday night."

"Well, you can make it until then. Miriam will get things straightened out when she gets home."

"Even if she does, it'll just be something else next month. It's not like Dale is going to wake up one morning, realize he's hateful, and change his ways."

"Maybe he'll die," she said hopefully. "Or maybe someone will knock him off, like in the movies. Say, wasn't Ralph Hodge in jail once? I bet he knows someone who can kill him."

"Don't you think that's a bit extreme?" Sam asked.

"Perhaps so, but let's not rule it out."

Sam made a mental note never to cross his mother.

He wished his mother a pleasant evening, hung up the phone, and went to bed. His mother, her curiosity stirred, looked up on Google how to kill people without getting caught.

11

While Gloria Gardner was reading about poisonous toadstools, the engine in Ellis Hodge's Ford pickup sputtered once, then twice, then died, stranding him and Miriam on Interstate 65, smack in the middle of the John F. Kennedy Memorial Bridge, spanning the Ohio River, connecting Indiana and Kentucky. Semitrucks blasted past them, rocking their Ford back and forth.

"Darn Democrats," Ellis muttered. "I knew this was bound to happen."

"What do the Democrats have to do with it?"

"It's a Democrat bridge," Ellis sputtered. "They've been laying for me."

"I told you fifty miles ago to get gas, but you didn't. Don't blame the Democrats for your poor judgment."

Within a few minutes, a police officer pulled up behind them, asked to see Ellis's driver's license, wrote him a ticket because it had expired the month before, then radioed a tow truck to bring a gallon of gas, which cost Ellis ninety dollars, the same amount he was trying to save by driving straight through and not getting a hotel room.

They pulled into their driveway a little after midnight, grateful to be home and not crushed in a tangle of metal over the Ohio River, while people inched past them in the left hand lane, slowing to view their mangled bodies.

"I'm never leaving the county ever again," Ellis said. "I've had it with travel."

He lay in bed, rehashing their trip, enumerating his many disappointments, from the price of gasoline to souvenirs made in China to state police and tow truck drivers, who he suspected were in cahoots and getting rich on unsuspecting tourists.

He finally fell asleep, but Miriam lay awake, thinking it might be time for Ellis to take up residence in the barn. Maybe set him up with a cot, a recliner, and a small refrigerator, like the one they bought for Amanda to take to college. Miriam never dreamed it would come to this, but it was either that or homicide and as a Quaker she was opposed to violence. Moving Ellis to the barn seemed the lesser evil.

So it was, that in the wee hours of a new day, two virtuous Christian women, Gloria Gardner and Miriam Hodge, were respectively contemplating how best to knock off one man and banish another.

12

Saturday morning found Sam Gardner at the Coffee Cup with his younger son, Addison, eating pancakes and listening to the gossip, much of it about him and how he'd lost his mind and broken the law marrying two women. The same Bob Miles who had lauded his kindness and courage was now predicting Sam would be arrested before the day was over.

"If you get sent to jail, can I have your car?" Addison asked.

"I'm not going to jail. They don't send people to jail for saying a prayer at a gay wedding."

"Wouldn't be so sure about that," Bob Miles said. "Down in Texas it's a life sentence."

"Maybe if a few more states started arresting a few of these liberal preachers, we'd nip this nonsense in the bud," Myron Farlow said. "I'll tell you right now, if my priest married two gays, he'd be gone in a heartbeat. I'd see to it."

Vinny Toricelli, the owner of the Coffee Cup, snorted. "Myron, I haven't seen you at church in so long you've probably forgotten how to get there."

"That doesn't mean I don't have my morals," Myron said.

"Good to know the owner of a bar has morals," Vinny said.

"Well, just see if I eat here anymore," Myron said, peeling a bill from his wallet, throwing it on the counter, and stalking out.

Dale Hinshaw, two booths down from Sam, finished his cup of coffee, paid his bill, then stopped at Sam's table on his way out. "Well, I hope you're proud of yourself. You've got the whole town fighting. That's a fine Christian witness."

Sam continued to eat his pancakes, ignoring Dale, who turned and left.

"Dale Hinshaw's a big, fat butthead," Addison said.

"Be nice," Sam said. "Just because he's rude, doesn't mean you have to be. Besides, he's not big. Neither is he fat."

It being Saturday, Barbara was working at the library, so after Sam and Addison finished eating, they stopped in to see her. She introduced them to Janet Woodrum, the new librarian.

"We've met, but haven't been formally introduced. Hello, Janet. It's a pleasure to have you in Harmony," Sam said, extending his hand. "Barbara thinks the world of you."

"Well, I think the world of her. I can't believe we have someone of her caliber working with us."

"We're very happy for her," Sam said.

"That's not what you said last night," Addison pointed out. "Last night you were complaining about having to do the extra cooking and housework."

There were days Sam regretted being a pacifist and today was shaping up to be one of those days. It wasn't yet ten o'clock, and he had already been tempted to wring several necks.

"I understand you pastor the Quaker meeting here in town," Janet said, deftly changing the subject.

"That's right," Sam said. "You're welcome to join us some Sunday."

"Thank you for asking, but I've been attending the Unitarian church."

You and half my meeting, Sam thought.

"She and Matt have a date tonight," Barbara said. "He's taking her up to the city to see a play."

"I guess that means he's feeling better," Sam said.

"Yes, much better," Janet said. "And it was so kind of you to step in and conduct Chris and Kelly's wedding at the last minute. They really appreciated it and so did Matt."

"I didn't actually conduct it," Sam said. "I just said a prayer."

"All the same, it was very kind of you. And brave."

"It got him in lots of trouble," Addison said. "Dale Hinshaw's trying to get him fired."

"Let's not talk about that now," Barbara said.

"Well, if the Quakers fire you, we Unitarians would love to have you," Janet said.

Sam was momentarily lost in thought, imagining what it might be like to pastor a Unitarian church. No more Dale Hinshaw dragging the church back to the Stone Age, no more Fern Hampton waging jihad against the Friendly Women's Circle, no more Bea Majors pounding the organ every Sunday morning until his eardrums exploded. They used guitars in the Unitarian church! Guitars and flutes, softly and expertly played, with hymns about nature and love and laying down your weapons and riding bicycles instead of driving everywhere. Hymns that actually matched the sermon theme and didn't consign people to hell in cheerful 4/4 time. The guitarists and flutists didn't miss half the notes and blame the congregation, like Bea Majors did each Sunday. He wondered how one went about becoming a Unitarian pastor.

When they arrived home, Addison changed into his sweats

and went to the park to shoot baskets. The message light on their answering machine was blinking. Miriam Hodge had phoned, informing him they'd returned early from their vacation and would see him the next morning at Quaker worship. "Call me if you need to talk," she said.

He debated whether to bother her. If he phoned her every time Dale Hinshaw was off his rocker, they'd be talking several times a day. He decided to let it rest, and went out to his garage to organize his nuts and bolts, a task that kept his hands busy and his mind free, permitting him to think grand thoughts and noble ventures.

13

The next morning, Barbara and Sam went to the meeting-house early to get the coffee started. Before long, Uly Grant arrived with the doughnuts, and folks began streaming in, including Deena Morrison and the Iverson family, with twins in tow, followed by Miriam and Ellis Hodge, who seemed especially cheerful to have survived their out-of-state ordeal and greeted everyone with robust hugs and a few tears.

"You wouldn't believe it down there," Ellis told Sam. "It's crazy."

"Well, I'm glad you're back home safe," Sam said. "It's good to see you, friend."

Sam fussed over the Iverson twins, gave them each a dough-nut, asked them about school, then predicted they'd be the first twins to serve as president of the United States.

"Don't be silly. They were born in China," Fern Hampton said. "They can't be president. It's against the Constitution."

Leave it to Fern to dash a child's dream.

The twins hurried off to their Sunday school class, while the adults gathered in a circle in the basement dining room. This was the worst hour of Sam's week, listening to Dale Hinshaw teach the adult Sunday school class. The class was reading its way through the Bible, a verse at a time. Dale would read each verse, stopping after each one to ask, "What do you suppose the Lord is trying to tell us here?" When anyone ventured a guess, he would argue with them. They had been in the book of Habakkuk for several weeks, hung up on the sixth verse of the first chapter, "For lo, I am rousing the Chaldeans, that bitter and hasty nation, who march through the breadth of the earth, to seize habitations not their own."

"Who are the Chaldeans today?" Dale asked. "What nation has set itself against God?"

No one dared answer, for fear of getting him cranked up.

"I would have to say it's the Soviet Union," Dale said. That the Soviet Union had gone belly-up decades before seemed not to have occurred to him, and he spent the next hour blaming every modern ill on a nation that no longer existed.

Sam excused himself to prepare for worship. Deena Morrison followed him out. "Boy, I didn't miss that," she said. "We either need a new teacher, or need to start a new class."

"Probably easier to start a new class," Sam said. "No way he's going to give up teaching that class."

"Maybe Judy Iverson and I can work on starting a new class," Deena said.

"That would be great," Sam said. "Run it by Jessie Peacock. She's the clerk of our Christian Education Committee. I imagine she'll be delighted to help you."

"Speaking of Jessie, I heard about Asa's heart attack. How's he doing?"

"I saw him the day before yesterday and he was feeling much better. I think they'll be back at meeting next Sunday."

"Maybe I'll take him a pie and talk to Jessie while I'm there," Deena said.

Sam hugged Deena. "I'm glad you're back," he said. "Barbara and I sure have missed you."

Sam had spent Saturday evening softening his sermon. A sermon that in its first writing had been a scorcher against intolerance and narrow-mindedness was, by the day of its delivery, reduced to a flickering candle, a general admonition to be nice to people and love everyone.

At the conclusion of worship, Dale stood, announced that the elders had called an emergency meeting of the church, and urged people to stay.

Gloria Gardner announced the profits of the Chicken Noodle Dinner, then reminded the ladies of the Friendly Women's Circle to gather Tuesday morning to begin making noodles for the next dinner.

Sam offered a closing prayer. He hadn't even said "Amen" before Miriam Hodge was hustling toward Dale. "What do you mean the elders called an emergency meeting? I'm the clerk of the elders and I wasn't aware of this."

"We sent out an e-mail this past Wednesday," Dale said. "Don't you read your e-mails? Something came up when you were gone and we had to meet. We've got ourselves a situation and people need to know about it."

Miriam was starting to remember why she didn't take vacations. The congregation was making its way to the basement for the meeting. It was out of her hands now.

Harvey Muldock was the clerk of the meeting. He was a nice man, good with furnaces and lawn mowers, but the finer distinctions of chairing a meeting were lost on him. He clerked a meeting like he drove—gas pedal to the floor, no brakes.

"Let's start with a prayer," Harvey said, after everyone had found a seat. The crowd fell silent. "Lord, we don't know why we're here, but you know why and we trust you to be with us and guide us. Amen."

"Amen," people rumbled.

Harvey turned to Miriam. "Miriam, you're the clerk of the elders. What's so important it couldn't wait until our regular meeting?"

"I have no idea. Ellis and I have been out of town. This meeting is a total surprise to me."

"Dale, what's going on here? Miriam's the clerk of the elders. The elders can't call a meeting of the church without her knowing about it."

"Says in *Faith and Practice* they can. If the clerk of the elders is unavailable, the elders can call a meeting. Miriam was out of town, but the rest of us could meet, so we did. We sent everyone an e-mail announcing today's meeting, and called the folks who don't have e-mail."

"Well, what's so all fire important it can't wait another week?" Harvey asked.

"Sam conducted a lesbian wedding," Dale said. "It says in *Faith and Practice* that marriage can only be between a man and a woman. And Sam knew that and did it anyway."

"Is that right, Sam? Did you marry two women?" Harvey asked.

"It was inadvertent," Sam explained. "I didn't realize they were both women until the service had started."

"Where was this wedding?" Harvey asked.

"At the Unitarian church," Sam said. "Their pastor got sick at the last moment, so I stepped in to help him. We ministers do that for one another in emergencies."

"The Unitarians don't have any rules against lesbian weddings, do they?" Harvey asked.

"Apparently not," Sam said.

"Well, then, I don't see the problem," Harvey said. "You weren't conducting a Quaker wedding. You were conducting a Unitarian wedding, so you had to go by their rules. If it's not against their rules, I don't see how we can fault you. Anybody else have a problem with Sam helping the Unitarians?"

"I think it's terrible," Fern snapped. "He needs to be fired."

Bea and Opal nodded their heads in agreement. Were it up to them, Sam would be blindfolded, given a last cigarette, stood against a wall, and shot.

"St. Ambrose said, 'When in Rome, do as the Romans do,'" Miriam Hodge observed.

"Well, if it's good enough for a saint, it's good enough for me," Harvey said. "Now, Sam, if you ever get sick and the Unitarian minister has to pinch-hit for you at a wedding, we would expect him to do things our way just like you did things their way," Harvey said.

"I'm sure he would," Sam said.

"Then that's that," Harvey said, standing up. "If we leave now, we'll get home in time for the Colts game. Meeting's over, folks."

"You can't end a meeting because of a football game," Dale protested. "You haven't given everyone a chance to talk."

"I don't see how sitting around flapping our jaws is going to help us one bit," Harvey said. Several people nodded their heads in agreement, all of them men who wanted to watch the game. "Looks like we're done then," Harvey said. "Thank you all for staying."

It was, according to Ellis Hodge, who had attended every

church meeting for the past seventy-two years, the shortest meeting ever held in the history of Harmony Friends Meeting.

While Sam was pleased with the outcome, he knew Dale Hinshaw would not go silently into the night, and that even now, in the dark and twisted recesses of his corrupted mind, the man was plotting Sam's pastoral demise.

14

The haste with which Deena Morrison began a new Sunday school class was staggering. By Sunday evening, she had secured Jessie Peacock's approval, drafted the help of half a dozen people, went online to research curriculum, narrowing it down to two possibilities: *God as She: A Perspective on Feminist Theology* and *The World's Religions: The Many Paths to God*. She phoned Judy Iverson for her opinion, who suggested Deena put it to an informal vote.

"Why don't we send out an e-mail to the meeting with a brief description of each class? See what people might be most interested in."

"That's a wonderful idea," Deena said. "If people have a say in it, they'll feel more invested."

Deena sent out a church-wide e-mail the next morning, on Sam's day off. Within fifteen minutes, he'd received four phone calls from irate Quakers threatening to jump ship. By the end of the day, *God as She* had gotten three votes, and *The World's Religions*, two. But eight people had voted to rescind Deena's membership in the meeting, fire Sam, and appoint a pastoral search committee.

At the meetinghouse, Lindsey Hinshaw had gotten a dozen phone calls, left at noon for lunch, hadn't come back, and wasn't planning to do so anytime soon. She left a message on Sam's answering machine to tell him she was quitting, that it wasn't worth the trouble.

"I don't know how you do this," she said in her message. "These people are driving me crazy. They're so uptight."

Barbara was working at the library. Sam spent the day there, reading a book on how to sell your own home. The nostalgia that had motivated the return to his childhood church was quickly fading. He was beginning to imagine what it might be like to start fresh somewhere else. He'd always wanted to own a hardware store in a small town and sell pocketknives and tools and other useful items. He'd never met a depressed hardware store owner. He and Barbara had visited the Bahamas for their twentieth anniversary. There were seven hundred islands in the Bahamas and surely one of those islands needed a hardware store.

He went home at lunch to eat a sandwich. He got four phone calls, but ignored them all. He had learned not to answer the phone or listen to his answering machine on his day off, lest he be plunged headlong into work. He started a load of laundry, then returned to the library.

"Are you going to spend the entire day here?" Barbara asked.

"I most certainly am," he said. "Not one person in the congregation knows I'm here. I might move in a cot and sleep in the periodicals."

He napped for an hour, read *National Geographic* cover to

cover, then talked with Janet the librarian about her relationship with Matt the Unitarian pastor. He advised her against marrying a pastor.

"It's no kind of life. You spend all your time helping people, but it's never enough. Plus, you have to work every weekend when your children are off from school. When you have time, they don't. When they have time, you don't."

"Matt probably won't stay a minister," Janet said. "What he really wants to do is teach."

"Well, there you go. Tell him to do it now, while he's young."

Barbara's shift ended at five, so they walked home together and made breakfast for supper—French toast and bacon—which boosted Sam's mood considerably. He loved breakfast food for supper and would have it every night were it up to him. After supper, they washed the dishes, folded laundry, and went for an evening walk, just the two of them. An empty-nest kind of evening, a portent of things to come.

They talked about the boys, then made plans to visit Levi in a few weeks, after he'd had time to settle in at college. Addison was still planning on joining the military, a prospect that alarmed them both. The Gardners were not warrior stock. They came from a long line of passive people who hated conflict, and now their younger son, their baby, was going to be yelled at by sergeants and taught how to knee people in the crotch. It depressed them to think about it, so they changed the subject.

"What are you going to do about Lindsey?" Barbara asked.

"What's wrong with Lindsey?"

"You didn't listen to the answering machine, did you?"

"Nope, not on my day off."

"She quit," Barbara said. "Said people were driving her crazy."

"Looks like the rats are jumping the ship," Sam said, grimly.

They walked in silence, thinking. After a few minutes, Sam said, "I probably should have hired Nora Nagle when I had the chance. I wonder if she would leave the Legal Grounds to come work at the meetinghouse."

"I heard Judy Iverson was looking for part-time work, now that the twins are in school," Barbara said, not caring one whit for the prospect of her husband spending time alone with Nora Nagle in the meetinghouse basement.

"She'd be great," Sam said. "You think she'd do it?"

"Never hurts to ask."

"I'll call her tomorrow."

They passed Sam's parents' house. His father was raking leaves in the near dark, so they helped him finish, then went on their way. All in all, it had been a fine day. The time off had given him perspective, and he fell to sleep thinking none of his problems were so great they couldn't be solved with intelligence, careful work, love, and forgiveness.

15

The end of Sam Gardner's ministry at Harmony Friends Meeting came with startling swiftness. Miriam Hodge delivered the news in Sam's office the next morning. She was seated on the couch when he arrived, a wad of soggy Kleenex in her hand.

"They've started a petition asking for your removal," she said.

"Who is they?" asked Sam.

"Dale, Fern, Bea, and Opal. All the elders but me. They've got a dozen signatures so far. Ordinarily I wouldn't worry about it, but they got Asa Peacock to sign it."

"Asa Peacock? Why would he want me gone? Asa and I are friends."

Not three years before, Sam had come back from vacation two days early to conduct the funeral for Asa's mother, who wasn't even a member of the meeting, and Asa repaid him by signing a petition to boot him out. Sam felt as if he'd been punched in the gut.

"I asked him why he signed it and he told me it was none of my business. He seemed very upset."

Sam sighed, sad breath leaking out of him.

"What are we going to do?" Miriam asked.

Sam sat quietly, collecting his thoughts.

"We're not going to do anything," he said, finally. "If after fourteen years I have to fight to keep my job, it's not worth it. I'm giving my notice."

"Oh, Sam, don't make any rash decisions. Go home and talk with Barbara before doing anything you might regret. You don't need to leave, and we don't want you to leave."

"Apparently a dozen people want me to leave," Sam said. He leaned back in his chair. "Miriam, I've grown cynical. All I do is complain about my job. I'm angry and negative all the time. I don't know if it's time for me to stop being a minister, but I think it's maybe time for me to stop being a minister here."

He drew a piece of paper from his desk and scrawled, *I, Sam Gardner, am resigning as the pastor of Harmony Friends Meeting, effective January 1st.* He slid the paper across the desk to Miriam. "Consider this my notice."

"Oh, Sam, don't do this. We can beat this."

"I don't think that would be good for me or the meeting," Sam said. "It's time."

"Please pray about it, Sam. We have time. When word gets out about this petition, people will be furious, and rightly so. You've been a wonderful pastor to us."

"Miriam, please don't tell anyone about this petition. Let it drop. I don't want the meeting fighting over me. Besides, they're probably right and I didn't want to give them the satisfaction by admitting it. It's time I went. I don't have the energy for it anymore. And with Addison wrapping up high school this year, he'll be gone. It's a good time for me to make a change, too."

Miriam left, still in tears. Sam began working on his sermon, but was too distracted, wondering what he would do. They had no savings to speak of. The year before they'd taken out a second mortgage to replace the roof. He wished his college degree had been in business, something that might actually generate an income. No, he'd majored in theology, the most useless degree ever devised. Theories about an ethereal being no one has seen for three thousand years. What had he been thinking? Maybe he could manage a dwindling enterprise on the brink of insolvency. He'd had plenty of experience with that.

At noon, he left the meetinghouse and walked home for lunch. The closer he drew to home, the more his resolve weakened. He waited until after lunch to tell Barbara he would soon be unemployed.

"I'm not surprised," she said. "I can tell your heart hasn't been in it."

"I'm tired," he said. "They deserve to have a pastor with some enthusiasm for the work."

"What were you thinking of doing?"

"I thought I might take some time off to catch my breath," Sam said.

Barbara had many fine traits, one of which was candor. "Have you seen our bank account? We have about two days for you to catch your breath, then you'll have to get a job."

"I was hoping I could take some time off for reflection," Sam said. "Maybe be a bit more intentional about what I should be doing for the second half of my life."

Barbara opened the most recent edition of the *Harmony Herald* and turned to the classifieds. "Hmm, let's see. Harvey Muldock needs a salesman at his Chevy dealership. You might go see Harvey. Here's a job where you can make two thousand dollars a week from your home. That's got to be a scam." She turned the page. "Eddy Plumbing over in Cartersburg is looking for an assistant. How do you feel about plumbing?"

"Not interested." Sam had never cared for physical labor of any sort.

"Are there any ads for a psychiatrist?" he asked. "I always thought that would be an interesting job."

"You don't know the first thing about psychiatry."

"I could learn."

"Not soon enough to do us any good."

Barbara returned to the paper. "They need a night clerk at the Speedway gas station in Cartersburg. It says benefits available."

"Sure, I'll take that job, and get shot my second night there and have to spend the rest of my life in a wheelchair eating Jell-O. That's a fine idea."

"Then I suggest you call Miriam and tell her you've reconsidered," Barbara said.

Sam was starting to wish he hadn't acted so hastily. He walked into the kitchen to phone Miriam, but her line was busy. He tried again in a few minutes, and Miriam picked up the phone. "Just calling to see how you're doing," Sam said.

"Better, thank you. I've phoned the elders and told them you've resigned. We've scheduled an emergency meeting for tonight to form a pastoral search committee."

That didn't take long, Sam thought. It had never been like the elders to move quickly any other time, but now they had the gas pedal pushed to the floor.

"And I've phoned the superintendent, and he's agreed to meet with us tonight," Miriam added.

"Sounds like things are moving right along," he said, increasingly alarmed. "Of course, if things don't work out, I guess I could stay if the meeting needed me to."

"That's awfully nice of you, Sam. But I thought about it some more on my way home, and I think you're right. A change might be a healthy thing for all of us."

From his counseling classes, Sam knew there were five stages of grief: denial, anger, bargaining, depression, and acceptance. It had taken Miriam roughly four hours to navigate all five stages. That had to be a record.

"I'm glad you're feeling better, Miriam."

"Yes, much better, thank you. One thing we're already starting to realize is that what we've been paying you isn't sufficient. Whoever we bring on board will need considerably more in terms of pay and benefits."

Sam wondered why that hadn't occurred to them before.

"Yes, I suppose you're right," he said. "Bills have a way of adding up."

"Don't want to give you the bum's rush, Sam, but I've got a few more calls to make."

"Of course, Miriam. Glad you're okay."

Being intentional about the second half of his life would have to wait. He phoned Harvey Muldock.

Harvey answered the phone. "Muldock Motors."

"Hi, Harvey. Sam here. Say, I read in the *Herald* that you were needing a new salesman. I might be interested."

Harvey laughed. "Don't be silly. You have a job. Hey, Sam, wish I had time to joke with you, but I'm busier than a one-eyed man at a go-go girl convention. Gotta go. See you Sunday."

Sam was thinking it would have been wise to have a new job lined up before quitting his old one.

He went upstairs to talk with Barbara. She was changing the sheets on their bed. He pulled on the fitted sheet, tugging it into place.

"Say, they wouldn't happen to have another opening at the library, would they?" he asked.

"Why do you ask?"

"Oh, I just thought it would be nice to work with you. We don't get to spend much time together what with me gone all the time."

"You can't get your job back, can you?"

"I think God might be telling me to take up a new line of work," Sam said.

"Oh, Sam. Don't get me wrong, I believe in you. But pastoring is the only thing you know."

"That's not true. Remember when the boys were in Cub Scouts and I helped them build their pinewood derby cars? I could do that. Or last summer when our car wouldn't start and I figured out what was wrong and fixed it. Remember that?"

"Sam, you left the lights on all night and the battery died. It wasn't rocket science."

"I was just pointing out that I'm good at other things besides pastoring."

"You're good at many things, Sam. You're a wonderful husband, a loving father and son. You're very creative. People respect you. But the only job you've ever had is pastoring. I know it drives you crazy sometimes, but I also know that most days you like being a pastor."

"It's all I know," he said.

"That is precisely my point," Barbara said. "Now, let's think. When did you tell them you'd leave."

"January first," he said, glumly. "I'm sorry, honey."

"There's nothing to apologize for," Barbara said. "You did what you thought was right. Now let's move forward, not look back."

Sam flopped down on the freshly made bed and began thinking aloud. "I heard the pastor at First Friends is retiring this July. I could always apply for that meeting."

"You'd want to live in the city?"

"Why not? It might be fun."

"I'm not sure you could live in the city. You break out in hives every time we go there. Besides, you always said you didn't want to pastor a large meeting where you couldn't get to know people."

"Hey, how about Salem Meeting? It's open," Sam said.

"Salem Meeting is always open. No one in their right mind wants to pastor there. We're not that desperate."

The phone rang, interrupting their speculations. Barbara answered, then passed the phone to Sam, mouthing the words "It's the superintendent."

As if the day weren't bad enough.

"Hello."

"Sam, this is your superintendent."

"Yes."

"I spoke with Miriam Hodge and she told me you've resigned."

"Yes, that's right."

"I knew you were going to call me to see about a job..."

"Actually, I wasn't planning on calling you," Sam interrupted. "Miriam told me she had informed you, so I thought that was sufficient."

"Well, if you had phoned me, I was going to tell you not to apply for another church in this yearly meeting. I've sent an e-mail to all the congregations announcing your resignation, explaining the circumstances, that you had, in direct violation of *Faith and Practice*, willfully conducted a same-gender marriage. I've asked them not to hire you."

"Thank you," Sam said. "That was very kind of you. You've saved me the trouble of applying to meetings for whom such a thing would matter."

"I hope you've learned a lesson from all of this," the superintendent said.

"Yes, the whole experience has been quite instructive. I've learned that some people are so small-minded they wouldn't extend even a crumb of grace to gays and lesbians. I don't know if that was the lesson you wanted me to learn, but that is the conclusion I have drawn. I have to go now; Barbara and I were discussing our future."

He hung up the phone, turned to Barbara, and said, "On the bright side, I will no longer have to deal with the superintendent."

"Things are looking up already, aren't they," Barbara said laughing.

Sam laughed with her, but inside he was broken. Though life as a pastor in his hometown sometimes frustrated him, this wasn't how he'd wanted his ministry here to end. He'd wanted to welcome infants into the world, see them through their school years, wave them off to college, join them in matrimony, then celebrate the birth of their babies. One full cycle. That had been his dream. He wanted people to talk about him with fondness and respect, the way they spoke about Pastor Taylor. He'd wanted a retirement party, with letters thanking him for his service, and a quilt given to him, hand-sewn by the Friendly Women's Circle. He'd wanted the superintendent to attend the party and shake his hand and thank him for all he had done. Instead, Dale and Fern had hounded him out, wearing him and everyone else down until the only hope for peace was for him to leave.

He stared at the ceiling. "What in the world am I going to do?"

16

Supper that night was quiet. They told Addison, who picked at his food, consumed with worry at the prospect of changing schools in his senior year.

"Don't you worry," Sam said. "Even if we have to move, you can always live with Grandma and Grandpa and finish school here. Everything will be fine." But the idea of being separated from his son made him nauseous.

At nine o'clock there was a knock on their door. Sam opened it to find Miriam Hodge standing on their porch.

"Hi, Sam. May I come in?" she asked.

"Certainly, Miriam. Come in, come in. Have a seat."

They sat in the front parlor.

Miriam fidgeted, clearly dreading the reason for her visit.

"What can I do for you?" asked Sam, helping her along.

"Um, Sam, the elders just met, and they feel it's best for you to leave now. I tried talking them out of it, but they think your continued presence will be divisive. They wouldn't budge. According to our contract, you're owed ninety days salary."

She pulled an envelope from her purse. "I guess they were

pretty sure of themselves. They already had the treasurer make out a severance check."

"Just like that? I can't come back and say good-bye? Who's going to preach this Sunday?"

"Dale and the superintendent have offered to preach until we call a new pastor."

"All of this because I said a prayer at a wedding for two women?"

"I'm sorry, Sam. This wasn't my idea."

Miriam pulled a crumpled Kleenex from her purse and blew her nose.

"Ellis and I will be leaving, too," she said. "I tendered our resignation at the end of the meeting."

"Oh, don't do that," Sam said. "You've gone there all your lives."

"We can't in good conscience stay. And I owe you an apology. I never should have accepted your resignation this morning. I don't know what I was thinking. I should have stood with you and fought it out. Please forgive me."

"There's nothing to forgive," Sam said. "You were doing what you thought was best for the meeting."

"What's best for the meeting is to not let bullies stomp and scream like spoiled brats until they get their way," Miriam said. "In that regard, I failed the meeting, and I failed you. I'm so sorry."

"This is all for the best," Sam said, not wanting to cause this kind woman further pain. "I think the meeting needs new leadership. Perhaps someone who didn't grow up here, who can come in with a clean slate. I hope you and Ellis will stay and help the new pastor along."

"That won't happen," Miriam said. "Ellis is furious. When

he found out Asa had signed the petition against you, he called him and yelled at him."

"That's exactly what I don't want. Ellis and Asa have been friends since childhood. Tell Ellis I've forgiven Asa, and he should, too."

They sat quietly, both of them thinking.

"You've been a wonderful pastor to us, Sam. When Ellis's brother Ralph was such a mess, drinking all the time, and we had to take in Amanda, you were so supportive. Ralph hasn't had a drink in five years, and Amanda's in college and doing well, and Ellis and his brother are back on good terms, all because of you. We're so grateful for all you've done."

"I'm grateful for you, Miriam. You've been a blessing to me and my family."

"You deserve better than this."

"You know, things always have a way of working out well for me," Sam said. "We're going to be just fine."

And saying it out loud, he believed it. With all his heart, he believed it. He wasn't sure what lay ahead, but he knew it would be good.

17

What do you mean, we owe Purdue five thousand dollars?" Sam bellowed. "We don't have five thousand dollars."

"It's for Levi's housing for the second semester," Barbara explained. "It has to be paid in advance."

"That's crazy! Where in the world are we going to find that kind of money?"

"You might remember my asking that very question last spring when we paid the first semester's housing. I said, 'Where will we get five thousand dollars in October for the next semester's housing?' and you said, and I quote, 'Don't worry, honey, God will provide.'"

"I really said that?"

"Several times," Barbara said.

"Well, then, I must have meant it. So let's see what happens."

"The next time you're speaking with God, you might mention that Purdue wants their money by the fifteenth."

"Why don't you tell God?"

"Because I'm not the one who spoke on God's behalf," Barbara pointed out.

Sam had been job-free, a term he preferred over unemployed, for a little over a week, with not one prospect in sight. He had applied for unemployment benefits only to discover ministers weren't eligible for assistance. Deena Morrison had given him a job at the Legal Grounds Coffee Shop, but on the first day he sneezed while carrying three grande mocha lattes, which he spilled on a group of red hat ladies, scalding them. Deena fired him as nicely as she could, gave him fifty dollars to ease him out the door, and suggested he contact Harvey Muldock about selling cars.

"I don't want to sell cars," he told Barbara that night. "I know I called Harvey before, but it seems like such a cliché, an unemployed minister selling cars. I was hoping for something a little more meaningful."

"Until something meaningful comes along, could you maybe do a load of laundry, and pick up around here a bit? I could use a little help." With Sam out of work, she was now working every day at the library.

He had taken to watching *Dr. Oz* on daytime television and thought of getting his own television show offering medical advice. While he had no formal medical training, his many years as a hypochondriac had left him well educated about various maladies. He'd made the mistake of mentioning his idea to Barbara.

"So I guess we've now left the realm of reality," she said.

"What do you mean by that?"

"I mean you have absolutely no credentials for giving anyone medical advice about anything. You have no training in that field."

"I'd like to think that being a pastor has taught me something about illness. Think of all the hospital visits I've made over the years."

"You're right, I didn't even think of that. Say, since you help count the offering each week, maybe you should apply to be the bank president. I hear Vernley Stout's retiring."

Sam thought for a moment, intrigued at the possibility. "Not a bad idea," he said. "Not a bad idea at all."

"Oh, for Pete's sake, Sam, get another church. There has to be some church somewhere looking for a new pastor."

"I've read the classifieds in *Quaker Life* for the past six issues. They've all found new pastors. Those that haven't don't want me. I've been blackballed."

"Have you phoned any of the other Quaker pastors? Maybe one of them is planning to change churches and you could get a foot in the door somewhere."

"Now there's an idea," Sam said.

He began phoning the pastors that very evening. Most of them were sympathetic, but none of them were especially helpful.

"I heard you did a same-gender wedding," said Scott Wagoner, a pastor who had attended seminary with Sam.

"It was an accident," Sam explained. "I didn't realize the groom was a bride."

"Did you explain that to the superintendent?"

"I tried, but he was in no mood to listen."

"Yeah, well, listening is not his strong suit," Scott said. "Boy, he sure has a bee in his bonnet over this. What did you do to him anyway? I've never seen him so worked up."

"I guess I didn't pay His Highness sufficient reverence."

They groused a bit longer about egotistical leaders, then

said good-bye. Sam went through the downstairs rooms turning off the lights, then climbed the stairs to bed. A headache was forming just behind his eyes. He would have to call Levi tomorrow and tell him they were out of money for college. The thought of it sickened him, his son leaving college to mop floors for minimum wage at the McDonald's by the interstate. It was all he could do not to cry.

18

Sam and Barbara were awakened by the telephone a little after six the next morning. Sam reached the phone on the fourth ring and grumbled hello.

"Sorry to call so early," Dale Hinshaw said. "But I didn't know what time you left for work."

"I have no work," Sam said. "I was fired. Remember?"

"Something's bound to turn up," Dale said. "God never gives us more than we can bear."

"Well now, if that were true, no one would ever commit suicide, would they, Dale?"

"It's no wonder you haven't found another job, with an attitude like that."

"What do you want, Dale?"

"We want our church key back. Miriam was supposed to get it from you, but she forgot."

"I'll put it in the meetinghouse mailbox," Sam said.

"Don't bother. I'll come by and get it in a few minutes."

"No, Dale. I don't want to see you. When I was your pastor,

I had to see you. But now that I'm no longer your pastor, I prefer not to see you. Don't come by."

His piece said, Sam hung up the phone.

"Good for you," Barbara said. "It's about time you told that old goat off."

Sam strutted around the bedroom, feeling manly for the first time in weeks. "That'll teach him to mess with me!"

Barbara laughed. "That's my guy!"

Sam looked at Barbara and wiggled his eyebrows.

"Is Addison still asleep?"

"I believe he is."

Barbara was fifteen minutes late for work that morning.

Sam was at the bank as soon as it opened. Vernley Stout ushered him into his office.

"How can I help you, Sam?"

"I'm checking to see how much equity we have in our home," Sam said.

"Well, I can't give you an exact figure, since we haven't had your home appraised. But I can tell you how much you still owe on your mortgage, and once you know what your house is worth, you'll have some idea of your equity."

Vernley began tapping on his computer.

"It says here you owe $123,278.62. That's if you were to pay it off today. But don't forget you took out that second mortgage to replace your roof. Come to think of it, we had the house appraised then. Let me see what it was worth then."

He tapped a few more buttons.

"Well, Sam, according to this you're in the hole about six thousand dollars. The recession really hit house values. You're not thinking of selling, are you?"

"Don't want to," said Sam. "But if I can't find a job here, I might have to."

"Hope it doesn't come to that," Vernley said. "That's a lovely old home you have there, Sam."

"I don't suppose I could borrow five thousand dollars for Levi's college this semester."

Vernley winced. "Not without a job, Sam. But you get a job and I'm sure we can do something to help you."

"Thank you just the same, Vernley. Thought it wouldn't hurt to ask."

"No, never hurts to ask." Vernley reached across the desk and shook Sam's hand. "You let me know if you can't make your mortgage payment. We can't loan you any more money, but we can let things slide a little while on your mortgage. Sometimes it takes us three or four months to realize someone's missed a mortgage payment."

"Appreciate that. Hopefully, it won't come to that."

He left the bank and walked down Main Street looking for NOW HIRING signs. Bob Miles at the *Herald* wanted a boy to deliver newspapers, and Kathy at the Kut-N-Kurl wished to employ someone to sweep up hair, but Sam was not yet that desperate.

He ate lunch at home to save money—bananas and peanut butter—then went online to read the classifieds. All the jobs were in the city, most of them in trades he knew nothing about. He cursed his theology degree again.

He spent a half hour after lunch talking to telemarketers. He'd never cared for telephone solicitation, but now that he had nothing to do, he appreciated the conversation. Though it was startling how many times a day people called to sell them something.

His copy of *The Christian Century* arrived in the afternoon mail. He read an article about the rampant growth of atheism, yet another social trend working against him, then applied for the seven pastoral jobs listed in the back of the magazine. For an hour in the late afternoon he thought of becoming a writer and even wrote the first page of a novel about a small-town minister who went crazy, murdered the church elders, and hid their bodies in the freezer in the church basement, where they froze stiff as boards and weren't discovered until the next September when the ladies of the church held their annual noodle dinner. Suspicion fell on the church secretary, who went to prison, while the pastor was given a raise for his exemplary service during the church's difficulties. It was a great deal of action for a one-page novel, so Sam began adding adjectives to spread things out a bit, and then Barbara came home, so he stopped for the day.

Addison came in just behind her, emptied the refrigerator, answered their questions with monosyllabic grunts, then went upstairs to do homework.

"Want to go out to eat?" Sam asked.

"We can't afford it. How about we make pancakes?"

"You cook, I'll clean up."

"Deal."

They ate in the living room, while watching *Jeopardy!* It depressed Sam to be reminded how little he knew.

"How come they never ask any theological questions?"

"Probably because the average person isn't smart enough to answer them," Barbara said, tactfully. "It takes an exceptional mind to understand such lofty matters."

Sam smiled, striving to remain modest.

"I applied for seven church jobs today," he informed her.

"None of them Quaker, and all of them out of state. Plus, Bob Miles is looking for a paperboy and the Kut-N-Kurl needs a hair sweeper. So how was your day?"

"Busy, but good. You'll never guess who just returned the sex book."

"Who?"

"Guess."

"Fern Hampton and Dale Hinshaw. Together."

"Ugh, gross," Barbara said. "Nope."

"Who?"

"Matt, the Unitarian pastor."

"I didn't think you could tell who was checking out what."

"Not if you blab it all over town. So keep it to yourself."

"I wonder why he's reading a book about sex," Sam mused.

"He said it was for a sermon series he's writing."

"If I were a Unitarian pastor, I'd still have a job," Sam observed.

"If you were a Unitarian pastor, they would have given you a raise."

Sam sighed.

After *Jeopardy!*, they cleaned up the kitchen, watched a *Seinfeld* rerun with Addison, then went to bed. Just as Sam and Barbara were drifting off to sleep, their telephone rang.

"Daggone it," Sam said, leaping from bed. "I bet it's a telephone solicitor. Or that knucklehead Dale. That man doesn't have the sense God gave a goose."

He picked up the telephone. "It's ten o'clock. What's so important it couldn't wait until tomorrow?"

An unfamiliar voice said, rather hesitantly, "My name is Wilson Roberts. I'm calling on behalf of—"

"No thanks, not interested," Sam said, then hung up the phone and returned to bed.

"Who was that?" Barbara asked.

"Oh, somebody trying to sell us something."

He lay awake for an hour, unable to sleep, thinking about the money he owed, the light of the moon casting ominous shadows across the room, like hands reaching out to throttle him.

19

Did you get the key back from Sam?" Bea Majors asked Dale Hinshaw at the elders' meeting. They were meeting twice a week now, organizing the pastoral search.

"He said he'd leave it in the meeting mailbox, but he hasn't," Dale reported. "If we don't get it by noon today, I'm calling the police."

Miriam Hodge had been gone from the church less than two days and things were already a mess. Dale Hinshaw had staged a coup, disbanded every committee but his, and seized the church's computer to review the giving records.

"Here's a list of who gave what to the church," he said, distributing a list of donors around the table. "Now we'll find out who really loves the Lord."

"The nerve of that Owen Stout," Opal Majors sniffed. "Strutting around here like he owns the place and he didn't give a hundred dollars last year."

"I had no idea Miriam and Ellis gave that much money," Bea Majors observed. "Look, Dale, they gave more than you did. Maybe we ought to try and get them back."

"They've gone over to Satan," Dale said. "Leave 'em be."

"Actually, I heard they were at the Methodist church this past Sunday," Opal said.

"Ellis's grandmother was a Methodist. I always knew he wouldn't stick with us," Bea said.

"Dale, I thought you said you'd give more this year since we hired your granddaughter," Opal asked.

"She was here less than a month and now she's quit."

"But you said when we hired her that you were going to put half her yearly salary in the plate that very week," Opal said. "I don't see it here. Do you see it, Bea?"

"That's nobody's business," Dale said. "That's between me and the Lord. Now let's get down to business. The superintendent has given me some résumés of ministers looking for jobs. Let's look them over."

"I don't want a woman preacher," Opal said. "It just doesn't seem right."

"The Bible is clear on that," Dale said. "First Corinthians, fourteenth chapter, thirty-fourth verse. Women are to be silent in church."

"I agree," said Bea Majors, who had never been silent in church or anywhere else.

"That leaves us three candidates. Two of them went to seminary. I don't want them."

"That's the last thing we need, another know-it-all," Opal said.

Dale scanned the remaining résumé. "Hey, this looks promising. This fella went to the Lester Hickam Bible College in Chattanooga. Paul Fletcher. Fifty-six years old. Good and seasoned. I bet he wouldn't marry two women. Named for an apostle, too."

"It says here he's pastored fourteen churches in ten years," Opal pointed out. "Should that worry us?"

"I bet he's not an ear-tickler," Dale said. "Probably preached the Word and people couldn't take it. I like the cut of his jib. Let's hire him."

"Shouldn't we interview him first?" Bea asked.

"Well, I suppose we can, but that would be relying on the wisdom of man instead of trusting the Holy Spirit," Dale said. "Are you doubting the Holy Spirit, Bea?"

"Oh, no."

"Then it's settled. Let's call him and see when he can start."

"Doesn't the rest of the church have to approve it?" Opal asked. "In the past, the whole church had to agree when we hired a new pastor."

"Where in the Bible does it say that?" Dale asked.

"It says so in our *Faith and Practice*," Opal said.

"Well, if you want to take man's word over God's word, that's your choice," Dale said. "But I know where I stand."

"Well, I guess it's all right, then," Opal said.

"How much are we going to pay him?" Bea asked.

"We'll ask him what he needs," Dale said. "But if he's the man of God I think he is, it won't matter to him. Do you think Billy Graham ever made people pay him before he preached to them? Did Jesus ever ask for money? I don't think so."

"Remember last year when Sam asked for a raise?" Bea said. "That didn't set well with me at all. It's like he wasn't trusting the Lord to provide."

"We're lucky to be shed of him," Dale said. "I think he was the main reason this church wasn't growing more."

They chewed on Sam another hour, then phoned Paul

Fletcher to tell him that after much prayer, the Lord had brought him to their attention.

Dale told him, "One minute we'd never heard of you, then the next minute it was like the Lord said, 'This is my servant, with whom I am well pleased.'"

"Well, let me tell you what happened, Brother Dale. Not one hour ago, the Lord Himself laid a burden on my heart for the town of Harmony. And I told the Lord, I said, 'Lord, if that's where you want me to go, that's where I'll go.'"

"Praise the Lord," Dale said.

They praised the Lord back and forth a few more minutes, agreed to pay Brother Paul ten thousand more dollars than Sam had ever made, then sent an e-mail to the meeting announcing the happy news.

20

He hung up on you?" Ruby Hopper asked Wilson Roberts. "Yes, before I could even tell him why I was calling. I told him my name, he said he wasn't interested, and he hung up the phone," Wilson explained.

"That's odd," Ruby said. "That doesn't sound like Sam. I've never actually met him, but the few times I've seen him at yearly meeting, he seemed cordial. Did you mention you were on a search committee?"

"I didn't have the chance."

Ruby Hopper and Wilson Roberts were seated at her kitchen table, surrounded by stacks of paperwork, eating gooseberry pie, drinking coffee, and trying to find a pastor.

"What do you think we should do?" Ruby asked. "Should we try phoning him again?"

"I don't see that we have much choice. No one else is willing to be our pastor."

"Have faith, Wilson. There's a Quaker minister somewhere who feels called to pastor a small meeting. We just have to find him. Or her."

The word *small* was a generous description. Hope Friends Meeting was down to a dozen people, all of them over sixty years old, most of whom had objected to the hiring of the current superintendent, and had consequently been ignored by him, which had troubled them at first, though they now believed it to be a blessing.

"What makes you think we can get this man to be our pastor?" Wilson asked.

"He's in trouble, just like us," Ruby said. "The superintendent has ordered meetings not to hire him."

"I like him already. What did he do to make the superintendent mad?"

"He was my cousin Miriam's pastor, and according to her he married two women."

"He's a bigamist?" Wilson asked.

"No, I mean he conducted the wedding for two women. But he didn't mean to. It was an accident. At least that's what Miriam said."

Wilson chuckled. "That's quite an accident."

"So no one will hire him. Care for another piece of pie?"

"Thank you, yes." Wilson Roberts had developed a noticeable paunch since starting their search for a pastor for Hope Friends Meeting.

Hope Friends had opened its doors in 1979, begun by twenty ambitious Quakers. They had met in the basement of a bank, then in a school gymnasium. Within a few years their numbers had swelled to over a hundred and fifty and Ruby Hopper had donated a piece of ground to the meeting, a ten-acre grove of beech and hickory trees. They had built a meetinghouse there, which proved to be their downfall. If they had kept things simple they would have become the largest Quaker meeting in the state. Instead, they fell victim to hubris, believing their growth was a result of their charm. They were now down to twelve Quakers. Twelve discouraged Quakers, all of whom were on the search committee when it began three years before. They had dropped off one by one, disheartened by the lack of progress. Wilson Roberts had stayed on for the pie and because of his secret infatuation with Ruby Hopper, and Ruby was still at it because she never quit anything.

So far they had interviewed eight pastors, who suddenly found opportunities elsewhere when they discovered the size of the meeting. Their last interview had been the month before, with a candidate who had spilled what appeared to be motor oil on his shirt and not bothered to clean it. Ruby could have forgiven that oversight, but he also had dirt under his fingernails, oily hair, and said the word *ain't* six times.

"I don't want to be a snob," Ruby Hopper told Wilson, "but is it too much to expect a pastoral candidate to take a bath? Tell me if I'm wrong, but I don't think I am."

A lesser woman would have given up, retired to Florida, and joined the Episcopalians, but Ruby held fast. She mowed the meetinghouse yard, kept the meetinghouse clean, and just the month before, at the age of seventy-five, had climbed up a ladder and cleaned the gutters. Wilson had held the ladder.

Wilson Roberts and Ruby Hopper had known each other since high school, when she was a looker. He had never married, hoping he and Ruby might end up together, though he failed to mention that possibility to her and she had married someone else, an accountant who was good with numbers but not so skilled at love. Or long-term commitments. While vacationing in North Carolina, he had waded into the ocean, began swimming east toward England, and was never seen again. For all she knew he had made it to England. Ruby had waited five years, then had him declared dead so she could sell his car.

It had happened decades before, but Wilson Roberts was not one to act in haste, and had been waiting for the right moment. He had been all set to ask her to dinner the day she cleaned the meetinghouse gutters, but the mood wasn't conducive to romance, so he put it off. He was hoping their search for a pastor would bring them together, that she might fall in love with him over a résumé and kiss him smack on the lips, but she'd managed to restrain herself.

Their monthly meeting of the pastoral search committee was winding down. Wilson was finishing his second piece of gooseberry pie and Ruby was writing out their next steps.

"I will call Sam today, and hopefully set up a time we can meet with him. Is there any day that isn't good for you?"

"I can do it any day," Wilson answered. "Delicious pie. It's not just anyone who can make a gooseberry pie."

"I'm glad you enjoyed it. Feel free to take the rest of it home with you."

She covered the pie with aluminum foil and ushered him to the door. He had begun lingering after their meetings, dropping hints about dinner. She was desperate to get another member on the committee so as not to be trapped alone with Wilson every time they met. She had even suggested they conduct their meetings over the telephone, but he had opposed the idea.

"Communication is more than words," he'd said. "I always told my salesmen that. Look a man in the eye when you're selling him a bathtub. You got to be able to read him. If I said that once, I said it a million times."

She could read Wilson Roberts's facial expressions, thank you very much, and didn't like what she was seeing. Having tried her hand at marriage, she wasn't eager to repeat it. Not even with Wilson Roberts, who had made a fortune selling plumbing fixtures, owned half a trailer park in Florida, and drove a top-of-the-line Cadillac, even though he was a Quaker and should have known better.

No sirree, Bob, no marriage for her. Not to a man who talked incessantly about bathtubs and sinks and shower stalls, whose idea of sophistication was a pink toilet. She was perfectly content, or at least would be once they hired a new pastor to help her kick this meeting in the pants and get it moving forward.

21

Sam was taking a nap when the telephone woke him up. He'd been up late the night before, unable to sleep after learning Harmony Friends Meeting had hired a new pastor. In the back of his mind, he'd nurtured the hope they might call him to say a mistake had been made, that they had acted in haste and wanted him to return to his job. But the hiring of Paul Fletcher had scuttled that possibility. The finality of his situation hit hard. His days of pastoring in his hometown were over. Maybe his chances of pastoring anywhere were over. He'd contacted a dozen churches that were looking to hire a minister and not one of them had bit.

He reached the kitchen phone on the fifth ring.

"Hello."

"Hello. Is this the Gardner residence?"

"Yes, it is."

"My name is Ruby Hopper and I'm calling—"

"Not interested. Take my name and number off your calling list, please."

"Wait, don't hang up. This isn't a sales call."

"Yeah, that's what they always say. I don't want to hear a sales pitch. I don't want to take a survey. I don't want to talk about insurance, credit cards, or mortgages. My roof is fine. I don't need new gutters. And my basement is dry."

"I didn't call about any of those things. I'm the clerk of the Hope Friends Meeting pastoral search committee, and am calling to see if you might be interested in talking with us about an opening we have."

An opening!

"Excuse me, what church are you from?" Sam asked.

"Hope Friends Meeting."

"Hope Friends Meeting," Sam repeated. "Oh, yes, you're up in the city, right?"

"Not right in the city," Ruby explained. "We're south of the airport, just outside the city. In the suburbs, actually."

"Yeah, I remember now. You're the ones with the meetinghouse in the beech trees. I went to an American Friends Service Committee meeting there about ten years ago."

"Yes, that's us."

"I thought you closed your doors," Sam said. "I haven't heard anything about you for a while."

"The superintendent is under the impression we don't matter, but I assure you we are very much alive."

Sam was suddenly intrigued. Any meeting on the wrong side of the superintendent had to be doing something right.

"We understand you've been let go by Harmony Meeting," Ruby said. "Is that right?"

"In a manner of speaking."

"Miriam Hodge is my first cousin. She explained your situation to me. We were hoping we could meet with you this week to discuss an opportunity for ministry. Perhaps tomorrow evening."

"I've been in touch with several churches," Sam said, which wasn't technically a lie, since he had, in fact, been in touch with several churches, though none had been in touch back. "Could I check my calendar and call you back?"

"You certainly may." She gave Sam her phone number, thanked him for his time, said good-bye, and hung up.

Sam hurried down the stairs, two steps at a time, to the junk drawer in the kitchen, where he found the book of statistics for Quaker meetings. Hope Friends Meeting...weekly attendance: twelve...annual pastoral salary, not much, but better than nothing. It beat sweeping hair at the Kut-N-Kurl.

But, geez, only twelve people, Sam thought. *How in the world can they afford a pastor?*

He waited an hour before calling Ruby back. No sense in letting her think he was desperate.

"Hello, Ruby Hopper. Sam Gardner here. I've managed to free up tomorrow evening, so I'll be happy to come your way. Would you like my wife to come, too?"

"That is entirely up to you. We would enjoy meeting her, but we are very aware that we're interviewing you, not her."

Sam was impressed. He had heard of churches who hired pastors without trotting their spouses through a dog-and-pony show, but had never personally encountered one.

"I will leave the decision to her," Sam said, though he had no intention of doing so. Barbara was going whether she wanted to or not. He would sooner take on a terrorist cell by himself than face a pastoral search committee without backup.

"In any event, we look forward to seeing you tomorrow evening, at seven o'clock, at our meetinghouse."

"See you then," Sam promised, happier, as his grandpa used to say, than a possum in a corncrib with the dog tied up.

22

He walked to the library to deliver the news to Barbara in person. She was in the fiction section, in the T's, organizing the Mark Twain books, and was less than enthusiastic when he told her the news.

"You mean I'll have to quit my job? I just got it," she said. "And Addison is in his senior year of high school. We can't ask him to move right now."

"I thought we'd discussed this," Sam said. "He was going to stay here with my parents."

"Then he graduates and joins the army and we don't see him for the next four years, plus we miss most of his last year of school. I'm not going to do that, Sam."

"Maybe I could move up there and start the job and you could move after Addison leaves. I could always come home on Sundays and Mondays."

"You would want to be away from us?"

"I don't want to, no. But I've been without a job for over a month now, and meetings aren't exactly lining up to hire me," Sam said. "I can't afford to be picky."

Barbara had dispensed with tidiness and in frustration was cramming Mark Twain books on the shelf every which way.

"What do you know about this meeting?" she said. "Hope Friends? I've never even heard of it. What do they pay? How many people attend? Can we even afford to move?"

"I don't know what they pay. I don't know their theology. I haven't even met them yet. I know the superintendent doesn't like them. That's probably a good sign. Come with me tomorrow night and we'll find out these things together."

He decided not to tell her that Hope Friends had only twelve members. Better she find that out gradually, preferably from someone else.

"Sam, I don't want to move. Our friends are here. Our family is here. Your parents aren't getting younger. They're going to need us more and more. And you want to move somewhere we don't know a soul."

"You didn't honestly think we could stay, did you?" Sam snapped. "Look around, Barbara. No one wants me. You think I want to be a paperboy again? Or sweep hair? There's nothing here for me. I can't even face people. I feel like a failure. As for our friends, most of them are in the church, and I don't see them standing up for me."

"Maybe you should have stayed on and fought it out," Barbara said, her voice rising. "Maybe if you hadn't given up so quickly, maybe our friends would have spoken up. They probably thought you wanted to leave."

The library had grown quiet. The patrons were listening, while pretending to read. This was better than any book, the former Quaker minister and his wife arguing in public. Two pacifists going at it like cats in heat.

"I can't talk about this right now," Barbara said. "I have to get back to work. Let's discuss it tonight."

"Fine," Sam barked, and stalked off.

After Sam left, Barbara went to the restroom to cry. She wasn't sure about her tears, whether they were sad or angry, and thought maybe a little of both. Sad and angry. Sad for their family and the strain they were under, angry at Sam for his odd mix of passivity and bullheadedness.

She washed the red from her face, then returned to the checkout desk.

"Are you okay?" her boss, Janet, asked.

"Sam wants us to pack up everything, and leave our son and family and friends behind so he can pastor a church in the city, and we're almost broke, but other than that, everything's fine."

Janet smiled sympathetically.

"He hasn't had any luck finding work, has he?" Janet asked.

"Not yet. But I've told him it will take time and to be patient."

"I'm not taking sides, but look at it from his point of view. He's been providing for you and the boys all these years, and now he's unable to. He's probably worried and depressed."

"I suppose you're right," Barbara conceded. "But if he were just patient, I'm sure something would come along here."

"I'm not so sure. There aren't that many jobs in these small towns, unless he wants to drive over to Cartersburg and work at Wal-Mart."

Barbara knew Janet was right, but she hated the thought of moving. Couldn't bear leaving behind the stretch of dining room wall where the boys' heights had been marked in pencil. Someone else would buy their house, move in, and paint over their lives. It made her almost gag to think about it.

23

It took five blocks for Sam to cool down. He rounded the corner to home and saw a police car parked in his driveway, its red light revolving. Bernie Rogers, the town's policeman since Sam's childhood, had retired. The town's new police officer, whom Sam hadn't met, was standing at Sam's front door. He was young and bald, wearing a bulletproof vest, and appeared itching to arrest someone. Sam immediately thought of his sons. *Lord, let them be safe*, he prayed.

"Are you Sam Gardner?" the officer asked as Sam approached.

"Yes," Sam said. "What's wrong? Are my sons okay?"

The officer pulled a notebook from his shirt pocket, flipped it open, then said, "A Mr. Dale Hinshaw has filed a complaint against you. He says you have church property you've not returned. A key. Is that right?"

"You're kidding me, right? Is this a joke?"

"Theft is never a joke, sir. Do you have the key?"

"Somewhere, I suppose. I can't find it. I haven't used it in years. We don't even lock the church door."

"Sir, I'll need you to give it to me."

"I just told you I don't know where it is."

"Are you refusing to return the key to its rightful owners?"

"No, I'm not refusing. Didn't you hear me? I don't know where it is. I've lost it. It's gone. If I had it, I would be happy to return it."

The top of the officer's head was turning red, the veins in his neck throbbing. Sam wondered why so many police officers shaved their heads.

"Don't you worry about sunburn with a head like that?" he asked the officer. "I'd wear a hat if I were you, or grow some hair. One or the other."

"Sir, I'm going to take you in. Please step over to my car."

"Take me in?" Sam screeched. "Take me in where? We don't even have a jail. What are you going to do? Lock me in the trunk of your car? Now you listen here, young man: I've lived in this town my entire life. I'm old enough to be your father. I'm not going anywhere but inside my house. Now step aside."

He was in the county jail in Cartersburg until the next morning. Barbara had phoned Owen Stout, who'd phoned the sheriff, who had called the state office of homeland security, who reduced the charges from terrorism to resisting arrest. Barbara found the meetinghouse key on top of the clothes dryer, where she had put it the year before after removing it from Sam's pants pocket. She had been after him forever to empty his pockets before tossing his dirty clothes in the hamper, but he never did, so she let him stew in jail overnight to contemplate his bad habits.

Barbara picked him up and took him to breakfast at the Cracker Barrel, though they couldn't afford it.

They sat drinking coffee, waiting for their food.

"So, jailbird, what time tonight is our interview at Hope Friends?" she asked.

"You're going?"

"Well, yes, I'm going. If you want us to pack up and move halfway across the state, you better believe I'm going."

"What about Addison's schooling?" Sam asked.

"I've never in all my life known Quakers to make a quick decision. I figure it will take them three months to decide whether or not to hire you, in which case Addison will only have two months left at school. I'll stay behind with him, get things packed up, sell the house, then come be with you after he graduates."

"I've been thinking about that. I don't like the idea of us being separated. If they can't wait until Addison is done with school, then I'll know it's not where I'm supposed to be. Besides, if he's going off to the army, I don't want to be gone from him, or you," Sam said. "I had a lot of time to think while I was in jail, and from now on my family comes first."

Barbara leaned across the table and kissed him.

"It feels great to be a free man again," Sam said, stretching his arms and inhaling deeply. "Though I must say, prison turned out to be a good thing for me. I learned a lot about myself."

"Then it was fifteen hours well spent," Barbara said.

"Seemed longer than that somehow."

"Did you meet anybody interesting?"

"Yeah, they put me in the same cell with a serial killer," Sam said. "You busted me out just in time."

"It was the least I could do. I'm sorry about yesterday. I should have been more understanding. I know you've been worried about finding work. Forgive me?"

"Nothing to forgive," Sam said. "I'm the one who should apologize for storming off like that. I shouldn't have just sprung this on you and expect you to drop everything and move."

"Well, unless someone dies and leaves us a lot of money, we're going to have to work. If Hope Meeting calls you to be their pastor, then that's where we'll go. Besides, I'll have a better chance of getting another job in the city."

"You're the best," Sam said. "Did I tell you I kept your picture next to my cot the whole time I was in jail? You were all I thought of."

"That's sweet."

Fifteen hours in jail had done Sam a world of good. Barbara made a mental note to have him arrested more often.

24

Sam was ironing a shirt for his interview when Addison arrived home from school.

"It was all over school that you got arrested," he told Sam. "The kids thought it was pretty cool that a minister got busted."

"I'm not exactly proud of it," Sam said.

"Is it true you punched a cop?"

"Most certainly not," Sam said. "I don't hit people."

Addison looked vaguely disappointed.

Sam finished his shirt, then took a damp washcloth to his navy blazer to wipe away Eunice Muldock's makeup. She hugged him every Sunday at church, leaving an imprint of her face on his blazer.

The drive to Hope was a pleasant one, past farms and through small, tidy towns. As Sam and Barbara approached the city, countryside gave way to suburbs, and traffic thickened.

"Ooh, an Arby's, let's eat there," Sam said. "You wouldn't believe how many times I thought of Arby's when I was in jail."

"Didn't you say you were thinking of me the whole time?" Barbara asked.

"I did. I thought of you and me sitting in Arby's eating roast beef sandwiches."

They ate, then went in search of Hope Friends Meeting, which took some time, because of Sam's poor sense of direction, and the Quakers' tendency toward modesty and their reluctance to announce their presence with a helpful sign. But they finally found the handsome wood and stone meetinghouse on a quiet side street, barely visible through the trees of what at first glance appeared to be a wooded park.

"Oh, it's beautiful," Barbara said.

"I had forgotten how beautiful," Sam said in agreement.

In the opposite direction stood a smaller building of similar design.

"I wonder if that's the parsonage?" Barbara asked.

"I believe it is."

"Oh my gosh. It's gorgeous. Look at all the trees. It's like living in the middle of a forest. It doesn't even feel like we're near a city."

"Dear Lord," Sam prayed. "Please let these people be normal."

They parked their car and walked, hand in hand, up to the meetinghouse.

"It looks good so far," Barbara said. "But if anyone here is named Hinshaw, I'm leaving. I'm standing up and walking out."

"I don't think Dale has any relatives at this meeting."

Hinshaws could be found at Quaker meetings throughout the Midwest. They metastasized like cancer, leeching on to host bodies and robbing them of life. Fortunately for Hope Friends, Hinshaws gravitated toward small towns and avoided the cities.

A dozen people were in the meetinghouse, seated around a table at the back of the meeting room. They rose to their feet when the Gardners entered.

Sam recognized Ruby Hopper, who looked just like her

cousin Miriam, and made his way to her, smiling, his hand outstretched. "You're Ruby Hopper."

"I am, indeed," she said. "And you're Sam Gardner."

"Yes, and this is my wife, Barbara," Sam said.

"It's a pleasure to meet you, Barbara. Can I get either one of you something to drink? We have coffee, tea, lemonade, and ice water. And pie. Coconut cream or strawberry rhubarb, whichever you prefer."

Sam preferred a piece of each and was on the verge of saying so, when Barbara smoothly intervened.

"Water is fine, thank you. And Sam will have coconut cream and I'll have strawberry rhubarb. That's very kind of you, Ruby. Thank you."

A tall man with a wild thatch of silver hair approached them, offering his hand. "Name's Hank Withers. Pleased to meet you." He shook Sam's hand, then turned it to study his fingernails.

"Clean fingernails. That's a good sign. The last fella we interviewed had dirty fingernails. Now personally, it didn't bother me too much, but the women didn't care for it."

"I bathe regularly," Sam said.

"Forgive my husband," an attractive older woman said. "He thinks Quaker honesty requires him to say every thought that comes to mind. My name is Norma Withers. It's a pleasure to have you with us."

Sam greeted her, and introduced Barbara.

"Have you been to our meeting before?" Norma Withers asked.

"Several years ago. I was here for a meeting of the American Friends Service Committee."

"Oh, yes, now I remember. That's where I've seen you. Ruby and I prepared the meal for that gathering."

"Lasagna, homemade Italian bread, and salad," Sam recalled. "With peach cobbler for dessert, if I'm not mistaken."

Sam remembered every church meal he had ever eaten, and often reminisced aloud about them. Barbara headed him off at the pass.

"This is such a lovely meetinghouse," she said.

"Thanks," Hank Withers said. "It was the only church I ever designed. I'm an architect. Or was. Retired now. They hired me to design it in 1983, built it in 1984. Norma and I came the very first Sunday and joined three weeks later. Biggest mistake I ever made. They still owed me a thousand dollars, but when I joined the meeting they asked me to donate the balance. Designed the parsonage, too. Didn't get one red cent for it."

Sam chuckled. "Yeah, we Quakers are sneaky that way," he said. "But you did a fine job. This is one of the prettiest meetinghouses I've ever seen."

"Now I'm clerk of the Limb Committee," Hank said.

"Limb Committee? What's a limb committee?" Sam asked.

"Just like it sounds. I'm in charge of making sure the tree limbs get picked up. Got a lot of trees here. If we didn't have a limb committee, the yard would be a mess."

"What other committees are there?" Sam asked.

"Well, let's see, we have the limb committee, the pie committee, the roof committee, the snow committee, the lawn-mowing committee, the kitchen committee, a funeral committee, a parsonage committee, and the pastoral search committee," Hank Withers said.

"Don't forget the peace committee," Norma Withers added. "And technically, we have an elders' committee, but it doesn't meet regularly."

"We had a wedding committee once, but we haven't had a

wedding in years," Hank said. "And we're thinking of starting an outreach committee to focus on the growth of our meeting."

Ruby Hopper served Sam and Barbara their pie, then urged everyone to take a seat. "As you know," she told the group, "this is Sam and Barbara Gardner. They have joined us this evening to help us discern whether we should call Sam to be our next pastor. Let's go around the circle and tell Sam and Barbara our names."

Sam ate his coconut cream pie and listened intently, trying to memorize each name. Meals he remembered, but names slipped away.

"Now that we've been properly introduced, let's proceed," Ruby Hopper said. "First I want to thank Sam and Barbara for driving all this way to be with us. Sam, would you mind telling us a bit about your ministry?"

"Happy to. Since graduating from seminary, I've pastored two meetings. I ministered in Illinois for several years, then fifteen or so years ago, we returned to my hometown, where I eventually became the pastor of Harmony Friends, my home meeting."

"And how did that ministry go?" Ruby asked.

"Generally well," said Sam. "We experienced some growth. There were some theological differences, but we managed to work through most of them."

"I heard you got canned," Hank Withers said.

A portly older man nodded in agreement. "Yep, that's what I heard."

Sam racked his brain, trying to remember the man's name. "Wilson Roberts, right?"

"Yes, that's right. Owner of Roberts' Fixtures, now retired."

"Well, let me speak to that," Sam said. "My departure was a mutual decision. Several of the elders thought it was best I leave, and rather than putting the meeting through a contentious fight, I decided it would be wise to turn in my notice."

"My cousin Miriam told me all about it," Ruby Hopper said.

"It was probably for the best," Sam said. "I had done all I could for the meeting. It was time for new leadership."

He hoped he sounded diplomatic, like a statesman, above the fray.

"So marrying two women didn't have anything to do with it?" Wilson Roberts asked.

"That certainly didn't help," Sam conceded. "But just to be clear, I didn't marry them. I said a prayer for them. I was pinch-hitting for a Unitarian pastor who was ill."

Most of the people nodded, poker-faced, refraining from comment, except for a man and woman who looked displeased. Sam tried to recall their names. Mink? Kink? Fink, that was it, the Finks. Leonard and Wanda Fink. Sam wondered if they were unhappy with what he had said, or generally unhappy with life. They looked as if they were having teeth extracted without anesthesia.

"When you're a pastor," Sam said, "you have to be able to sense the end of your usefulness. You have to know when you've done all you can for a congregation. I didn't want to leave Harmony under these circumstances. I had hoped for a tidier end, maybe a party with cake, and a farewell sermon, but it didn't work out that way. Now we must discern together if I have the gifts you need to help this meeting forward, so let's focus on that."

"Well stated," said Norma Withers. "Let's discuss your thoughts on various matters."

They lobbed him a few softballs, which he answered easily. Questions about his spiritual journey, his education, his strengths as a pastor, his philosophy of ministry.

"Sam and Barbara, do you have anything you wish to ask us?" Ruby Hopper asked.

"I would like to know if you have certain expectations for the pastor's spouse," Barbara said. "Would I be expected to teach a Sunday school class or work with children or clerk a committee?"

"If you join our meeting, we would urge you to be open and faithful to whatever ministry God is calling you to. There will be no added expectations just because you're married to our pastor. Pastoring is his calling, not yours," Ruby explained.

Barbara never dreamed she would hear those words uttered. She began mentally packing up their house in Harmony, filling out change of address cards, and digging up her flower bulbs to bring with them.

"It's not that I don't mind helping in the meeting," Barbara hastened to add. "As a matter of fact, I enjoy working with children."

"About that," Wilson Roberts said, "we don't exactly have many children in the meeting right now."

"Well, wherever two or three are gathered—" Barbara began.

"We don't even have two or three," Norma Withers said. "In fact, we don't have any children here. We used to have a lot of children, but they've all grown up or left. We were hoping our new pastor, whoever that might be, could help us reach out to young families."

"Children are our future," Sam said. Whenever he was nervous, he was prone to utter tired, obvious clichés. He had wanted to break the news of Hope's size to Barbara gently. Maybe get a glass or two of wine in her first, get her relaxed.

"Heck, at this point, we'd take just about anybody," Hank Withers said. "Young, old, comatose. Anyone. We're not picky."

"If you don't mind my asking," said Barbara, who was going to ask whether they minded or not, "just how many people are in the meeting?"

"You're looking at it, sister," Hank said. "Everyone in the meeting serves on the search committee."

"Lately, it's just been Ruby and me," said Wilson Roberts.

"That's because we trusted you and Ruby to bring us a good candidate, and you succeeded," Norma Withers said, smiling. "Shifting gears a bit. Sam, this is a bit embarrassing, but it's the world we live in today. We will have to have a background check run on you. It's our policy for anyone seeking leadership in our meeting, or anyone working with children." She paused, then added, "Even though we don't have any children yet, we know that will change."

"I think background checks are wise," Sam said. "I don't mind at all."

In fact, at the recommendation of their insurance company, Sam had suggested the same thing at Harmony, but Fern Hampton had thrown a fit. "You're telling me I have to have a background check? That's outrageous. I was a public school teacher for forty-five years, and now you're telling me I'm a pervert. That's a fine how-do-you-do. You sure didn't care about my background when you asked me to teach Sunday school last year. Now you want to call the police to see if I'm a rapist."

Sam had dropped the subject.

"Before we end our time together, does anyone have any questions they'd like to ask Sam?" Ruby Hopper said.

"I'd like to ask Barbara a question," Wanda Fink said.

Wanda Fink had plucked her eyebrows, then had drawn them in with eyeliner high above her eyes, like the Gateway Arch, making her appear perpetually surprised. Her lips were pursed, as if drawn tight by a surgery gone wrong. She was a hard person to read.

"Yes," Barbara said, "what's your question?"

"I'm the clerk of the parsonage committee and one of our pastors' wives used an abrasive cleaner on the bathtub, even though I had distinctly warned her not to. What type of cleaner do you intend to use on the sinks and tub?"

There's one in every church, Barbara thought.

"It's probably premature to be talking about cleaning the parsonage, but if you decide to call Sam to be your pastor, and if he decides to come, then perhaps the parsonage committee can supply the proper cleaner," Barbara said with a smile, resisting the urge to reach across the table and smack Wanda Fink upside the head.

"Yes, let's leave it at that for now," Ruby Hopper said. "Sam and Barbara, thank you so much for being with us. I've made you a little something to take with you."

She hurried over to the refrigerator and pulled a pie from it. "I hope you like raisin pie," she said.

"We certainly do," said Sam. "That's very kind of you."

He turned to the congregation. "It was a pleasure meeting all of you. I do hope we have the opportunity to see one another again."

The twelve walked them to the front door and bid them good-bye.

"We'll be in touch," Ruby Hopper promised.

Sam opened Barbara's car door, just in case they were being watched, then hurried around to his side and pulled away from the meetinghouse toward Harmony.

25

So when did you plan on telling me there were only twelve people in the entire congregation?" Barbara asked, as they turned left out of the meetinghouse lane.

"Is that how many people are in the meeting?" Sam asked. "I really hadn't noticed."

"How in the world can a meeting with only twelve people stay open?" Barbara asked. "I don't see how they can keep it going. Are you sure we should do this?"

"They haven't extended an offer yet," Sam pointed out.

"They will. They want you."

"I don't think the Finks were all that smitten with me," Sam said.

"Yeah, she sure was uptight. Asking me about bathtub cleaner. What a kook."

"The pie sure was good. I'd become their pastor just for the pie."

"That's another thing," Barbara said. "Don't they seem kind of weird about pie? I mean, come on, a pie committee? I've never heard of a church having a pie committee."

"That is one committee meeting I wouldn't mind attending," Sam said.

They arrived home a little before midnight. Addison was still awake, awaiting their return.

"Are we moving?" he asked.

"Don't know yet," Sam said. "They'll probably want to think about it for a little while. Maybe have me back for some more meetings. Knowing Quakers they won't make a decision until this time next year."

"If you move before school is over, I want to go with you," Addison said.

Sam and Barbara looked at him, perplexed.

"Honey, we weren't going to move until your schooling was done," Sam said. "We'd already made up our minds about that."

"Besides, don't you want to graduate with your class?" Barbara asked. "You've been with them since kindergarten."

"Yeah, but some of them are jerks," Addison said.

"Got those in every group," Barbara said. "But it's not like you to say that. Did something happen at school today?"

He didn't answer at first, then said, "Nothing I can't handle."

"What's going on, buddy?" Sam asked.

"Dad, why'd you have to go and marry two women? Didn't you know it would cause us trouble?"

"Has someone been giving you grief about it?" Sam asked.

"Not at first, but now there's some guys who won't shut up about it." Addison's voice caught. "They called me a fag." He looked away, embarrassed.

"You want me to talk to the principal?" Barbara asked him.

"God, no," Addison said, horrified at the prospect of his

mother showing up at school. "I'll take care of it. Promise me you won't say anything."

Sam's heart ached for his son. He'd always tried to protect his children from cruelty and ignorance. Now this. It always came to this. Small-minded bullies, spewing out the garbage they heard at home, making life miserable for good and decent people.

"I'm sorry," Sam said. "Not sorry I did a kindness for two women who needed a kindness, but sorry the fallout spilled over onto you."

"Can I ask who they are?" Barbara said.

"Evan Farlow, and his cousin Landon."

"Isn't Evan the son of Myron Farlow?" Barbara asked Sam.

"Yeah. Myron was the same way when he was a kid. Meaner than a box of snakes."

"I know Evan," Barbara said. "He wanted to check out the sex book from the library." She was quickly losing all sense of confidentiality.

"Addison, no matter where you live, you're going to meet people who aren't kind," Sam said. "You can't let them wear you down. Go back to school, hold your head up, and ignore them. You have lots of friends. Stick with them."

"Yeah, well, some of them didn't like you marrying two women, either," Addison said.

"That's okay," Sam said. "People can disagree with one another, and still be friends."

"I'm not sure I want to be friends with them anymore."

"Don't be hasty. This is a new thing for some people. Give them time to sort it out," Sam advised.

Barbara went upstairs while Sam and Addison sat at the

kitchen table eating Cocoa Puffs, which made them both feel better.

"Nothing like a little partially hydrogenated vegetable oil and artificial flavoring to set things right," Addison said, reading the box.

"They do have a way of curing what ails you," Sam said, in happy agreement.

26

It had been so long since Sam had interviewed for a job, he'd forgotten the protocol. He couldn't remember whether he was to call them, or they were to call him. He was a nervous wreck waiting to hear from Ruby Hopper.

"I wonder if she's misplaced my phone number," Sam told Barbara. "Maybe I should call her."

"Don't do that. Ruby Hopper said she would be in touch with you. Give them time. I'm sure they haven't forgotten you. You know how Quakers are. It takes them forever to make a decision on a pastor."

"Dale Hinshaw and Fern Hampton found a new pastor in ten minutes," Sam said.

"That's because they're idiots," Barbara said. "And it's not going to last. He'll be gone by this time next year. I'm actually glad Hope is making this move carefully. It's a big step, for them and for us."

A week after the interview, late one evening, Ruby Hopper finally phoned. "I'm sorry it's taken us so long to respond," she told Sam. "The truth is, we've run into a bit of a snag and aren't sure how to resolve it."

"Perhaps I can help," Sam said.

"It's about your criminal record. I mentioned to you we'd be doing a background check."

"Yes, I remember you saying that."

"It seems you've been charged with resisting arrest," Ruby said. "I'm sure there's a perfectly reasonable explanation, but it has several of the people here concerned."

"There's a perfectly reasonable explanation," Sam explained. "One of the elders at Harmony Meeting phoned the police after I neglected to return my key to the meetinghouse. When the police came to talk with me, I was a bit abrupt and the officer arrested me. It was a big misunderstanding."

"The papers we were sent said you were under investigation by Homeland Security," Ruby said. "What can you tell us about that?"

"As I said, it was all a mistake. The police officer was a bit exuberant."

"It says in the report you called him a bald-headed fascist."

"Did I? I might have, but I don't remember that."

"Some on the committee are concerned it shows a lack of judgment," Ruby said.

"It was not one of my finer moments," Sam said. "I had told the elders I had lost my key to the meetinghouse, but one of the elders apparently didn't believe me."

"I called my cousin Miriam and she told me as much, and said it amounted to nothing. But you can see why it might give us pause."

"Yes, I understand. It would concern me, too."

"I'm grateful for the clarification," Ruby said. "I'll share what you've told me with the committee."

"I'd be happy to come up there and tell them myself, if you think it would help."

"I don't think that will be necessary," Ruby said. "It seems pretty straightforward. I'll be back in touch with you by tomorrow or the next day. I'm almost certain it will be good news. We were very impressed with you and Barbara."

"That's wonderful. I'm looking forward to hearing from you again."

Sam hung up the phone, then went in search of Barbara to tell her the news.

"Did I actually call the policeman a bald-headed fascist?" he asked her.

"Apparently, among other things," Barbara said. "When I came to pick you up, he mentioned a few of them. You kind of lost it that day."

"I think it was fourteen years of pent-up hostility all coming out at once."

"I hope you've apologized to that young man."

"Not yet. But I will. Tomorrow. I promise."

He did it the first thing the next morning, right after breakfast. Walked the four blocks to the town hall, and into the police room, found it empty, so went to the Coffee Cup, and found the officer sitting at the counter, still bald, drinking coffee and eating a cinnamon roll. Sam apologized for losing his temper, paid for the officer's coffee and pastry, and promised that if he were ever arrested again, he would go quietly and not call anyone names.

He stopped by the Unitarian church to visit with Matt, and told him about his interview at Hope Meeting and their fascination with pie.

"It's a weird thing about Quakers," Sam mused. "The meeting here in town is all about chicken and noodles, and this new meeting is all worked up about pies. I've never seen anything like it. Are Unitarians that way?"

"We have a lot of vegans and vegetarians," Matt said. "The pitch-in dinners here are god-awful. Thirty tofu dishes, and not one piece of fried chicken anywhere. You know I grew up Southern Baptist?"

"Yes, I remember you telling me that."

Matt sighed wistfully. "Now there was a group of folks who knew how to have a pitch-in. Fried chicken, pot roast, mashed potatoes, macaroni and cheese, apple pie, green beans, baked beans, soup beans. Sometimes I regret leaving them."

"So why did you?"

"They kind of helped me along. I was pastoring a church and appointed a woman to be a deacon. Asked her after church one Sunday and was fired before the day was out."

They commiserated over their various terminations, then Sam took his leave, walking around town. With the increased prospect of leaving his hometown, he was feeling kinder toward it, more willing to forgive its shortcomings. He was even starting to feel an odd sympathy for Dale Hinshaw, suspecting the pastoral tenure of Paul Fletcher would be both brief and nasty, and Dale would be blamed. Not that he didn't deserve blame, but Sam felt bad for him nonetheless. It was easy to feel charitable toward someone he no longer had to see on a regular basis.

He stopped at the library and checked out a murder mystery.

"Ooh, that's a good one," Janet Woodrum commented. "Lots of gore. A rather peculiar choice for a Quaker pastor."

"A currently unemployed Quaker pastor," Sam said, "and

therefore free to read whatever he wishes. I might even check out the sex book after Matt returns it."

"Which he might not do for some time. Considering how popular that book is, I may need to order another copy."

"Speaking of Matt, are you and he getting married?"

"Not that I'm aware of."

"I think maybe you should ask him to marry you," Sam suggested. "Women do that these days, you know."

"Just last week you told me not to marry a minister. You said it was no kind of life."

"Did I say that? I don't recall saying that. Why would I have said that?"

"I believe you told me ministers were too nosy and didn't mind their own business."

"Well, there you go," Sam said. "Consider yourself warned."

"Oh, before I forget. Barbara mentioned your interview at Hope Friends. I grew up very near that church. In fact, the Girl Scout group I belonged to met there."

"Talk about a small world."

"My parents still live there," Janet added. "Dad just retired. He was a doctor. My mom still works. She's a principal at one of the local elementary schools."

"Do your parents have a church home?" Sam asked, trying not to sound too eager at the prospect of a potential convert.

"Is that all you ministers ever think about?"

"Yeah, pretty much."

"As a matter of fact, they do have a church, but they're not happy there."

"That's wonderful," Sam said. "Are they miserable enough to leave and go somewhere else, say for instance a Quaker meeting?"

"I don't know," Janet said, "but I will certainly let them know you might be moving to their neighborhood."

Sam finished checking out his book, and walked home, elated. A brand-new murder mystery to read and two potential converts to a church he hadn't yet begun to pastor. A doctor and a school principal. People with brains. It was shaping up to be a fine day.

27

Christmas came and went. No longer in charge of the annual progressive nativity scene, Sam was able to relax and enjoy the season. Uly Grant had hired him to help out at the hardware store for the Christmas rush, and had kept him on. Ruby Hopper phoned each week to report the progress of the search committee. They were nearing a decision, and were down to working out the details—salary, vacation, health-care benefits, and the like. With the economy back on track, Wilson Roberts had sold off his interest in his plumbing fixtures business and donated a chunk of money to the meeting, causing Sam to be deeply grateful for toilets and sinks.

"I'll never say another bad thing about toilets as long as I live," he told Barbara.

There was an ice storm in March, knocking out power to the town for three days. With no Internet or television, families were forced to talk with one another. On the second day, cell phones lost their charge; people who had canceled their landlines were in a disconnected daze. Paul Fletcher preached a sermon on the end times, believing the loss of electricity was a portent of Christ's return, possibly within the next week or so. But the Son of Man didn't get the memo, so peace and quiet descended instead, and people began to wonder why they wanted television, Internet, and cell phones in the first place.

The last week of March, Addison Gardner departed from his customary gentleness long enough to punch Evan Farlow squarely on the nose, which earned him a three-day suspension. Sam took three days off from the hardware store and he and Addison drove to Gettysburg and stood on Little Round Top, where in 1863, Colonel Joshua Chamberlain and the men of the 20th Maine held fast against the rebels. In his mind's eye, Sam saw young men scattered dead upon the hills and began to leak tears, thinking of Addison leaving in a few short months to join the army. He had signed up the month before, had been sworn in, and would be leaving home at the end of June for basic training. Sam had always believed in letting his sons choose their own paths, but the thought of his younger boy being in harm's way was sometimes more than he could bear.

Levi was well along in his second semester of college. Barbara's folks, bless their hearts, had dug deep and helped, and Levi had gotten a job waiting tables on the weekends. He had switched his major from engineering to sociology, an interesting field of study, but no more lucrative than theology. Inmates making license plates earned more money than sociology majors. Sam figured his son would be financially better off in prison—three squares a day, free clothes, a cot to sleep on, and a little walking-around money. He tried not to think how much it was costing to subject his son to a lifetime of poverty. Sam had taken to playing the lottery, sneaking over to Cartersburg once a week and buying two dollars' worth of tickets, all for naught.

When he and Addison arrived home from Gettysburg, there was a message from Ruby Hopper on their answering machine, asking Sam to call her, which he promptly did.

"Can you begin the first of July?" she asked, by way of greeting.

"I certainly can," said Sam. "Our younger son is leaving for the army at the end of June, and we want to spend as much time with him as we can, but I think I can be ready by July."

Ruby Hopper laughed. "We've been without a pastor so long, another month won't matter. Why don't you enjoy time with your son, use July to pack and move, and start here the first of August?"

"That sounds perfect," Sam said. "I must say I'm a little surprised you decided to call me as your pastor. When it took so long, I thought you'd decided to go with someone else."

"No, it was nearly unanimous."

Nearly unanimous. Sam wondered who didn't want him.

"But it's all settled now, and you're going to be our new pastor. We have a few housekeeping details to take care of. We'd like you to select paint colors for the parsonage, so it can be painted before you move in. Perhaps you and Barbara would like to make one more visit, so you could walk through the parsonage."

"You're going to paint the parsonage?"

"Of course. Why wouldn't we?"

"I don't know," Sam said. "I just thought we would have to do that."

"No, you pick the colors you want, and we hire a painter. That's our responsibility. And you'll need to pick new carpet for the master bedroom. The kitchen has a stone floor, and all the other rooms have hickory floors. The master bedroom has carpet that probably needs to be replaced. Since you'll be living there, you should select the color."

Sam was beginning to think this was an elaborate practical joke. A Quaker meeting letting their pastor pick paint colors? Not just slopping white paint on everything and saying, "Good enough." Replacing the bedroom carpet before it was worn through? What kind of madness was this?

28

They drove to Hope the next day, before the meeting changed its mind. Hank Withers and Ruby Hopper met them at the parsonage.

"It's a beautiful house," Hank Withers said, opening the door to let them in. "I should probably be more modest since I designed it, but the truth is the truth. I was at the top of my game with this one."

Hickory beams spanned the living room and kitchen. A stone fireplace dominated one wall.

"Cut those beams from trees right here on the property," he said. "And those stones for the fireplace came out of the creek on the east side of the property. Hauled 'em up here myself. Of course, I was younger then."

A large screened-in porch sat off the kitchen.

"I worried the porch would make the kitchen dark, so I raised the kitchen ceiling and put in that row of windows above the roof of the porch. Gives you all kind of natural light in the kitchen," Hank said.

Sam and Barbara were too stunned to speak.

"When we asked Hank to design it, we told him we wanted it to reflect Quaker simplicity," Ruby Hopper said. "So he tried to keep it practical and use local materials as much as possible."

"The countertops are Bedford limestone," Hank said. "I come in every year and seal them. Just takes a few hours. The floors are hickory. Again, from trees we removed when we built the meetinghouse and parsonage."

"It's amazing," Barbara said. "I've never seen such a lovely home."

"The paint colors are fine," Sam said. "We wouldn't change a thing."

They walked into the master bedroom.

"This carpet looks perfectly good," Barbara said. "You don't need to replace it."

"If you change your mind, you let us know," Ruby said. "We want you to be happy."

They returned to the kitchen.

"If you have your own appliances and prefer to use them, we can put these in storage," Ruby said.

"We'd just as soon not have to move ours up here, so if you don't mind, we'll use these," Barbara said. "They look brand-new."

"A little over a year old," Hank said.

The Gardners' stove had two broken burners, the oven burnt everything, and the freezer built up a three-inch coating of frost every couple of months, which Sam had to chop out with a hatchet.

Sam and Barbara began measuring the rooms, to see what of their furniture could fit where. With the boys gone, there was no need to move all their belongings, so they had been planning a garage sale. Normally, Sam didn't care for people snooping through their things, but he could endure it this one time if it meant less stuff he would have to pack, haul a hundred miles, and unpack.

He stretched a tape measure across the living room, scribbled a figure in his notebook, then stuck his head in the fireplace and looked up the chimney.

"Does the fireplace work?" he asked Hank.

"Like a charm," Hank said. "We have a chimney sweep come every fall to clean and inspect it. As for the firewood, we try to stay on top of the fallen trees on the meetinghouse property. We'll cut it up and stack it for you. That's the limb committee's job."

"We'll give you a list of local contractors you can phone if anything in the parsonage needs to be fixed," Ruby Hopper added. "Plumber, electrician, painter, roofer, whatever help you might need. You just call them yourself, since you know your schedule. If you have any questions, you can ask Wanda Fink. She's the clerk of the parsonage committee. She couldn't be here today."

Ruby handed them several keys to the parsonage. "You can begin moving in whenever it's convenient for you."

"I have a chandelier that came from my grandmother's house," Barbara said. "We have it over our kitchen table. Could we put it in the kitchen here?"

"You just bring it right along. I'll make sure it gets hung," Hank said.

Ruby Hopper walked to the door. "We'll leave you alone to finish looking things over," she said. "Just lock up when you leave."

They shook hands good-bye, then Sam and Barbara walked from room to room, planning and admiring, then exited the house, securing the door behind them.

29

The traffic was light. Within a few moments they were in the open country, moving quickly along.

"I don't know about you, but I could move tomorrow," Sam said.

"Let's get Addison on his way first, then we can concentrate on moving."

"I'm sorry you have to give up your job," Sam said. "I know you enjoyed it."

"Maybe I can find a new one when we get settled. I don't want to just sit at home."

Sitting at home sounded highly desirable to Sam. He couldn't imagine why anyone might object to that.

They drove in silence a little while, then Sam began wondering aloud who at Hope had objected to his becoming the new pastor.

"I don't think it was Hank or Ruby," he said. "They seem very glad we're there. I wonder if it was that Wilson Roberts man?"

"I suspect it was the Finks, but it really doesn't matter," Barbara answered. "Don't dwell on it."

"I just wish I knew."

"I'm glad you don't know, then you'd try to win them over, and it never works. Just be yourself, be kind to all, and do your job. And stop at Kroger's. We need milk and bananas."

A half hour later they approached Harmony and turned into the Kroger parking lot.

"Is that the Peacocks' car?" Sam asked.

"Yes, I believe it is."

"Let's come back later. I don't want to see Asa."

Barbara reached over and thwacked Sam on the ear, hard. "Listen up, mister, you need to forgive him and move on."

"Ouch, I hate it when you hit my ear."

"Then don't be stupid and I won't. Asa Peacock was nothing but kind to you for fourteen years. When he and Jessie won the lottery, you got that nice bonus. Who do you think made that possible? Then he does one thing you don't like, he signs a petition, probably because he was hounded to death by Dale Hinshaw, and you won't talk to him. Now you go in that store with me, and act like the Christian you claim to be."

Asa and Jessie Peacock were leaving the store just as Sam and Barbara were entering it. Both couples stopped, and stared at each other for a moment. Jessie spoke first.

"Hi, Sam. Hello, Barbara. How are you, friends?"

"Hi, Jessie," Sam replied. "We're fine." He looked at Asa, then blurted, "Asa, I thought you were my friend. Why did you sign a petition to get me fired?"

"Oh, my Lord," Barbara said. "Is there not one ounce of tact in that thick head of yours?" She reached up to flick his ear again, but Sam was quicker and moved out of reach.

"It's okay, Barbara. I owe him an explanation," Asa said. "Sam, the truth is I got mad at you for marrying those two women. I don't have nothing against those people, but I don't think they ought to be allowed to marry one another. It doesn't seem right to me."

"I don't agree with him," Jessie said. "That's why I didn't sign the petition." She turned toward her husband. "And will you please stop referring to them as 'those people.' They are humans just like us."

"Why didn't you come and talk to me?" Sam asked Asa. "We could have discussed it. That's what friends do."

"Because I didn't want you talking me out of it, that's why," Asa said. "I've got my mind made up on that issue and I'm not changing it."

"You didn't have to agree with me, Asa. I've told you that before. Just because I say or do something, doesn't mean you have to agree with me. I respect your right to think differently from me. Remember that time you came to talk to me about the war, you knew I was against it, but we talked it through? We could have talked about this."

"You are talking as if this all rested on Asa," Barbara said. "You just as easily could have gone to Asa and spoken with him."

"Two stubborn men," Jessie said. "Walking around mad and depressed rather than swallowing a little pride and speaking to one another."

"I guess maybe I could have come talked to you," Sam said.

"Nope, that was my job to do," Asa said. "I owed it to you to work it out with you and I didn't. I'm sorry, Sam. I hope you'll forgive me."

"Of course I forgive you."

Asa reached out his hand, but Sam walked forward and embraced him.

"We are a mess, the two of us," Sam said.

"I sure do miss you, Sam. I was telling Jessie just the other day that our new pastor is a kook. No one likes him. Not even Dale. And everyone is mad at Dale and Fern and Opal and Bea for getting you fired. There's talk of removing them from the elders' committee. Miriam and Ellis have left. I tell you the whole place is a mess."

"I'm sorry to hear that," Sam said, though not entirely sorry. Maybe one day he would be entirely sorry, but for the time being he thought they deserved to be a little miserable.

They chatted a few more minutes, getting caught up on meeting gossip. Sam told them he would be pastoring Hope Friends Meeting, which made Jessie and Asa glum.

"I guess this means if the meeting asked you back, you wouldn't come," Asa said.

"No," said Sam. "I've given them my word. We'll be moving up there the tail end of July."

"I wouldn't blame you if you never came back," Jessie said. "You're probably glad to be shed of us after the way you were treated."

"Oh, no. We'll miss everyone. And with Mom and Dad still here, we'll be back from time to time," Sam explained. "In fact, when we come back, let's all go out for dinner. Us, and you, and my folks."

Asa beamed. "That sounds fine. We'll look forward to that."

They chatted a bit longer, then parted company. Sam bought a package of Oreos, which he and Addison ate that very night, down to the last broken piece at the back of the package.

30

Spring hurtled by. The days lengthened, the peonies lining the driveway bloomed, the trees glowed an effervescent, shiny green. The high school graduation was held the last Friday of May, and all the town turned out to witness it. Eighty-four graduates, their parents, grandparents, aunts, uncles, friends, and neighbors applauding them in the same sweltering gymnasium where Sam had graduated decades before. The strains of "Pomp and Circumstance" were wafting through the air, nearly overcome by the ancient stench of sweat, body odor, and athletic defeat. It was difficult to feel positive in a gymnasium that had been the site of so many humiliating losses, but they managed.

Barbara's parents were in town for the graduation, Levi was back from Purdue, and everyone gathered at the house for cake, ice cream, and presents. Sam gave Addison a Case pocketknife and Barbara, hoping to civilize her son, presented him with hardback copies of Thoreau's *Walden* and Whitman's *Leaves of Grass*, for which he seemed grateful. The grandparents presented him with two crisp hundred-dollar bills and Sam's dad told the story of how Sam had barely graduated from high school, ranking 77th out of 78 in the class of 1979, a story Sam had never told his children, and would have preferred to have kept from them, but there was no stopping his father.

At eleven o'clock, they called it a day. Barbara's parents were staying with Sam's mother and father, the Super 8 at the interstate being full. Barbara worked the next day, as did Levi, who had been hired by Ellis Hodge to scrape and paint his outbuildings. They went upstairs to bed, while Sam and Addison retired to the porch swing, where Sam told him about Hope Friends Meeting, and Addison explained the workings of the M-16 rifle.

"How do you know so much about the M-16 rifle?" Sam asked.

"I looked it up on the Internet."

Sam sighed. "I wish Al Gore had never invented the Internet," he said. "I almost didn't vote for him because of that."

"I think I'm a Republican," Addison said.

"Oh, my Lord. Don't tell your mother. She'll faint dead away."

They swung back and forth in a gentle arc.

"So when did you decide to join the army?" Sam asked.

"When I was twelve."

"Why didn't you tell us sooner?"

"I didn't want you to talk me out of it," Addison said. "I know how you feel about war."

"You're right," Sam said. "I don't like war, but I love you, which means I will give you the freedom to make your own adult choices. That said, I would be much happier if you went to college, became a doctor, and supported your loving parents in their old age."

"Do you think you'll move back here once you retire?" Addison asked.

"Haven't thought that far ahead. I guess it depends on how much we like it up there, and where you boys settle. We'd like to be near the both of you. Especially if you do your family duty and produce grandchildren we can spoil rotten."

A police car drove by.

"Is that the officer you attacked?" Addison asked. "You know, for someone who doesn't like war, you can be pretty violent."

"I didn't attack him. I was upset and called him something I shouldn't have. But I apologized and bought him a cinnamon roll."

"Well, he couldn't ask for more than that."

"I didn't think so," said Sam.

It was late; the day had been full, and momentous.

"I'm awfully proud of you, Son," Sam said. "I'm going to miss you like crazy."

"Miss you too, Dad."

Sam stood, took Addison's head in his hands, bent over, and kissed his son's forehead.

"You are a joy to me, Son."

They went upstairs, Addison to his room, and Sam to his, where his lovely wife lay, dreaming dreams.

31

They held their garage sale the middle weekend of June. Sam was a keeper, and Barbara was a thrower-away. They spent the week before the sale bickering and negotiating. Sam promised to dispose of his three-wheeled lawn mower if he could keep the wagon wheel passed down from his great-great-great-grandfather. It was said to be from the covered wagon the family came west in, in 1827, all the way from Cincinnati. Fifty miles of flat prairie ground, which they covered in three days, there being no major rivers to cross. They had been aiming for California, but got as far as Harmony, where they renounced their Lutheran faith and joined up with the Quakers. They had been there ever since, stagnating.

Sam's father came by the first morning of the sale.

"You're selling this?" he asked, incredulous, holding up a shovel with a cracked blade. "You can take this over to Ernie Matthews's and have him weld that blade. You'd think you were made of money."

"Or you can buy it from me for twenty-five cents and take it to Ernie yourself," Sam suggested.

"You'd charge your own father a quarter for this?"

"How about twenty cents?"

Sam and his father bickered back and forth before agreeing on fifteen cents.

"Can you believe Barbara wanted me to sell our wagon wheel?" Sam told his father.

"You're kidding me! The family wagon wheel?"

"The very one," Sam said. "She has no regard for history."

Barbara toyed with the idea of buying the shovel herself and smacking them both on the head.

The sale was wildly successful, Harmony being a small town and people liking nothing more than snooping through one another's belongings. Townspeople still talked about how Harvey Muldock's brother, Howard, sold off his collection of girlie magazines in 1982. When his dalliance with smut became public knowledge, he was booted out of the church, and had to close his business and move to the city, where people were accustomed to decadence.

But there were no such secrets in the Gardners' sale, just some old tools and children's videos, some of Sam's old clothes that no longer fit, Tupperware permanently stained with microwaved tomato sauce, and a smattering of pictures and plaques with Scripture verses that Sam had been given over the years. Three this-is-the-day-the-Lord-hath-made, two for-God-so-loved-the-world, and one the-wages-of-sin-is-death Scripture plaque, which Dale Hinshaw had given him the year before, after Sam had preached a sermon series on forgiveness.

The sale began at 8 a.m., and by 2:30 p.m. they were cleaned out. Harvey Muldock came past as they were folding the tables and putting them away, studied the wagon wheel, then offered Sam one hundred dollars, which Sam declined.

"I'm saving it for my sons," Sam said, and was promptly informed by his sons they wanted nothing to do with it, so Sam sold that, too, since Harvey was his third cousin, twice removed, and therefore practically family.

In all they made $126, which didn't seem worth the effort, but it gave them the excuse to get rid of things that would have otherwise cluttered their lives, so it was worthwhile. Sam divided the money between his sons, sixty-three dollars apiece.

"That's the closest thing you'll ever get to an inheritance," he told them. "Invest it wisely."

The next morning they left on their last family vacation. Camping, the only trip they could afford. They left their cell phones at home and drove four hours north to Lake Michigan, where they pitched their tent in a state park, perhaps the last remaining tent in the entire state. It was hot and humid and everyone else was camping in air-conditioned RVs, hooked up to cable television.

"That isn't camping," Sam said. "They might as well have stayed home."

They cooked over a campfire, bacon and eggs and Dinty Moore beef stew, and drank tepid lemonade. At night they roasted marshmallows and slapped mosquitoes and reminisced about past vacations, then spread out their sleeping bags on the tent floor and fell to sleep, hot and dirty but indescribably happy.

When the boys were younger, maybe even just a few years before, they would have whined the whole time, but now they were old enough to appreciate their last family vacation. One evening they drove to the nearest town and watched a movie at a drive-in theater, a thriller about terrorists seizing the White House and being thwarted by a minister from Iowa who had brought his family to Washington, D.C., to see the sights. The minister, it turns out, had once been a Navy SEAL, but had told no one, not even his wife, so everyone was surprised when he single-handedly rendered three dozen terrorists unconscious with a variety of jujitsu moves.

Sam, having on several occasions imagined himself doing much the same thing, loved the movie.

"That's the thing about us ministers," he told his family that night in their tent. "There are things we learned in our former lives that we can't talk about. They lie just beneath the surface, ready to be used should we ever need them."

"You told us you had always been a pastor," Addison said.

"You were too young to know the truth," Sam said. "Suffice it to say that I've done things I can't talk about. Secrets from long ago, before I met your mother. Matters too painful to talk about, that were utterly necessary at the time. I suppose I became a pastor to make up in some small way for the things I once had to do for my nation."

"Oh, brother," Barbara said.

Levi and Addison wanted desperately to believe their father was more interesting than he appeared, so they believed him. For the most part. They believed he had once done things he preferred not to talk about. It might even have been something exciting. Something involving espionage. Probably not, but one never knew.

They camped ten days, then returned so Addison could say good-bye to his friends before shipping out for basic training in Oklahoma. They drove him to the recruiter's office in Cartersburg the last day of June. Addison had given his family strict instructions not to cry in front of the recruiter, so they bravely shook his hand good-bye, his mother hugged him, then they returned to their car, where Sam began to sob.

"He's never coming home," Sam wailed. "We'll never see him again."

"Don't say that," Barbara snapped. "You want to jinx him?"

"Did Dad cry like this when I went away to college?" Levi asked from the backseat.

"All the way home," Barbara said. "He was distraught. We had to pull over several times."

Levi smiled, pleased his departure was the cause of parental sorrow.

"I was thinking," he said, "that with Addison gone for the next four years, I could maybe turn his bedroom into a game room."

"You'll have to take that up with the new owners," Barbara said. "We're moving next month. Remember?"

"Besides, you'll be back to college in a month's time," Sam pointed out, his voice catching. "Both our little boys, gone."

Sam could barely see to drive, so he pulled over to let Barbara take the wheel.

They began to pack as soon as they reached home. Sam borrowed Uly Grant's truck from the hardware store and began filling it with their belongings. They started in the attic, hauling boxes of Christmas decorations down two flights of stairs and out to the truck. After a few hours, Sam suggested they burn the house down and start all over, fresh.

"We'd probably make a profit," he pointed out. "That's the nice thing about a fire. It destroys all the evidence. We could tell them we lost a Picasso and get an extra half a million."

"I'm sure our insurance company would believe we owned a Picasso," Barbara said.

It took them two days to work their way through the attic, with numerous runs to the dump and a trip to the Amvets in

Cartersburg. They moved on to the basement, which had a tendency to fill with water so had been kept mostly empty. They boxed up Addison's things, then hauled the first load up to the city to the parsonage. Hank and Norma Withers met them there and helped them unload the truck, then took them to eat supper at Arby's.

"So I heard you go to Purdue?" Hank commented to Levi.

"Yes, sir. I'm a Boilermaker."

"Went to Ohio State myself. Studied architecture. What's your major?"

"It was engineering, then I switched to sociology. But I have a buddy who's an acting major, so I'm thinking of doing that."

This was news to Sam and Barbara, who tried not to act surprised.

"Lot of money in acting," Hank Withers said. "If you hit it big. Of course, most actors don't. They end up waiting tables. Not that there's anything wrong with waiting tables. Did it myself during college."

"I was also thinking of maybe majoring in engineering again. I kind of miss it."

Hank nodded. "A noble profession, engineering. If it weren't for engineers, we'd still be living in caves and pooping outdoors."

"Yeah, we engineers are pretty much responsible for modern civilization," Levi said, now proudly numbering himself among that accomplished tribe.

After dinner, they bid a warm good-bye to Hank and Norma, then returned to the parsonage. With no television, Levi took it upon himself to regale them with stories of engineering's finer moments in history.

"Herbert Hoover was an engineer. Did you know that, Dad?"

"No, I surely didn't."

"And a president, and a Quaker," Levi added. "We engineers are multifaceted."

It had been a long day, and before long Sam and Barbara fell to sleep on their air mattress while Levi spoke of splendid and sundry wonders.

32

The Gardners moved to Hope the last Friday of July. The day before they had met at Owen Stout's law office for the closing, where Uly Grant and his wife presented them with a check for their house, then raised their right hands and pledged not to paint over the strip of paint in the dining room where Sam and Barbara had recorded their sons' heights. That evening, the Hodges, Muldocks, and Peacocks stopped by with supper and lingered into the dark hours, visiting on the porch. Miriam and Ellis had returned to the meeting after the Methodists had attempted to baptize them. Ellis and Asa were reconciled, united in their mutual distrust of their new pastor, Paul Fletcher, who in a few short months had reduced Harmony Friends Meeting to half its former size.

Everyone was glum, except for the Gardners, who were trying, for the sake of their guests, to appear miserable.

"If it doesn't work out, perhaps you could come back," Miriam suggested.

"Thank you," Barbara said. "That's very kind of you."

Not on your life, Sam thought.

The past several months without Dale Hinshaw and Fern Hampton in his life had been pure ecstasy, as if he had been the test subject of some exotic narcotic. He had never known such elation. It had taken a few months for Sam to relax, for the trauma to wear off. He felt as if someone had been beating his head with a hammer, then had suddenly stopped. Feeling was coming back. And joy. His creative juices were bubbling again as he contemplated the twelve Quakers in Hope. Jesus had once accomplished wonders with twelve people. He couldn't help but wonder if the same might be true for him.

With their beds packed away in Uly Grant's truck, they slept at Sam's parents' house on the foldout sofa. Levi slept in the recliner. Sam's mother was beside herself with grief.

"We'll never see you again," she wailed, as they stood beside the truck the next morning, hugging one another good-bye.

"For God's sake, they're only moving two hours away. We can see them every weekend, if we want," Sam's father pointed out.

Oh, dear Lord, please don't let my parents visit every weekend, Sam prayed.

While there were some things he would miss about living in Harmony, being his parents' pastor wasn't one of them. On several occasions, in the middle of a sermon, his father had interrupted him in order to regale the congregation with a story, usually unflattering, from Sam's childhood.

Like the time Sam was preaching on marital love and his father had chuckled out loud from the fourth row and said, "Hey, Sam. Remember when you were fourteen or fifteen and we found that girlie magazine you had hidden under your mattress? Your mother was worried you'd end up becoming a pervert, but now here you are, a minister. Just shows you what the Lord can do."

Sam wouldn't miss that. Nor would he miss his mother rising to his defense in the monthly business meetings, including the time she told Dale Hinshaw he was so stupid he couldn't find his ass with both hands. Had actually said the word *ass* during a church meeting. His own mother. No, he wouldn't miss that.

Sam, Barbara, and Levi climbed in the truck, then swung past Uly Grant's house; Uly would follow them in their car to Hope, help them unload, then drive his truck back to Harmony that evening. With Levi driving, it took them a little under two hours to reach the outskirts of the city. Barbara sat in the middle, her legs straddling the transmission hump, and Sam stationed himself at the passenger window, cramming an imaginary brake pedal to the floor and yelling at Levi to drive slower.

Wanda and Leonard Fink were at the parsonage when they arrived, watering the daylilies and hydrangeas.

"Who are those old sourpusses?" Levi asked.

"That, my son, is Leonard and Wanda Fink," Sam said. "If I'm not mistaken, they are the people who didn't want the meeting to hire me as their pastor."

"You don't know that," Barbara said. "Now be nice, the both of you, or I'll send you back to Harmony and I'll stay here."

While the Gardners and Uly unloaded the truck, Wanda Fink hovered over Barbara, explaining the rules regarding the use of the parsonage, down to the hangers she preferred the Gardners use should they decide to display pictures on their walls, which she hoped they wouldn't since it left holes in the drywall that would eventually have to be spackled and repainted.

"The last pastor we had hung pictures everywhere," Wanda Fink complained. "It was an absolute disaster. It took the parsonage committee an entire afternoon to patch the walls. And he didn't put felt pads on his chair legs even though we told him to several times. There were several scratches on the floors. Inconsiderate. Just plain inconsiderate."

After she was done advising Barbara on matters inside the house, Wanda started in on Sam about the outside, recommending he mow north-to-south lines one week, and east to west the next. "We had a pastor once who mowed the same direction all the time. After a while the grass all leaned one way. And be sure the grass is never cut shorter than four inches. Otherwise, the weeds take over. And if you see moles, let us know immediately. One year we had moles and the yard was practically destroyed before the pastor told us." She shuddered at the memory.

"If we get moles, should I tell the parsonage committee or the lawn committee?" Sam asked.

"To hear the lawn committee tell it, you'd think it was their job," Wanda Fink said. "But as the clerk of the parsonage committee, I believe that's under my authority. The lawn committee thinks otherwise."

Sam was beginning to understand why Hope Friends Meeting was down to twelve people. If he had his way, it would soon be down to ten, with the Finks down the road at the Baptist church, giving some other pastor ulcers.

Sam promised to mow the yard in alternating directions, and Barbara pledged not to drive nails into the walls without permission. So Wanda Fink left satisfied, her husband in tow.

"I don't envy you this church," Uly said.

"She can't be any worse than Dale and Fern," Sam said. "And there's only one of her. Everyone else seems pretty nice. I can handle one kook."

It took them the rest of the afternoon, then Ruby Hopper

and Wilson Roberts stopped by with supper to give the official welcome. A woman was with them who looked vaguely familiar, though Sam couldn't remember her name.

"I'm sorry," Sam said, reaching out to shake her hand. "I know we've met, but I can't remember your name."

She smiled and Sam tingled. She wore her hair in a French braid, Sam's one weakness, and had a summer tan, Sam's second weakness, and deep blue eyes, his third.

"I'm Ruby's niece. You know my aunt Miriam and uncle Ellis. We met one Sunday several years ago when I was visiting them for the weekend and came to meeting with them. My name is Gretchen Weber."

As soon as she said her name, Sam remembered. Years ago, he had spent a half hour of Quaker silence admiring her surreptitiously until Barbara had noticed and cleared her throat, bringing him out of his reverie. She had raised the matter afterward, with Sam feigning ignorance.

"I'm not sure who you're talking about," he'd said. "I can barely remember her. You say she was with Miriam and Ellis? I don't even remember her name. Georgina? Geneva? Gail?"

Barbara had flicked his ear then, too.

Now here Gretchen Weber was again. Sam glanced at her left hand. No ring.

"Do you live in the area?" Sam asked.

"Less than a mile from here," Gretchen said. "I have a veterinary practice."

"Oh, that's right. I remember Miriam and Ellis telling me you were a veterinarian. Is Hope Friends your home meeting?"

"When I go to church, I come here, but it's not very often. My work takes up most of my time."

Sam was ready to invite her to attend regularly, when Barbara materialized at his side, took Sam's hand, and squeezed it until his knuckles cracked.

"Hello, Gretchen," she said. "It's so good to see you again. Isn't it nice to see Gretchen again, Sam?"

"It certainly is," Sam agreed, suspecting he was in trouble no matter what he said.

"This is our older son, Levi," Barbara said, introducing Levi to Gretchen. "And this is our friend Uly Grant. He's helping us move."

"Pleasure to meet you," Uly said. Yes, indeed, a great pleasure. Uly was grateful his wife wasn't there to crack his knuckles.

The food was carried in and their guests departed—Ruby, Wilson, and Gretchen to their homes and Uly back to Harmony, with the effusive thanks of the Gardners, who promised to keep in touch.

"Well," said Sam to Barbara, as Uly backed his truck out of the driveway, "it sure was nice of them to bring us dinner. Very thoughtful. And that Gracie seems like a nice young lady."

"It's Gretchen, not Gracie," Barbara said. "And stop acting like you're not attracted to her. We've been married nearly thirty years. I can read you like a dime-store novel, Sam Gardner."

"I only thought she was pretty because she reminds me of you," Sam said, ever the diplomat.

They ate supper, then began unloading their boxes, deciding what went where.

"It's odd not having Addison around," Sam said.

"Yeah, I kind of miss the little nerd," Levi added.

"I wonder what he's doing this very moment," Barbara mused. "I hope the sergeants aren't beating him up."

"I don't think they're allowed to do that," Sam said. "But whatever he's doing, I'm sure he's enjoying himself."

33

⌒

At the very moment, at Fort Sill, in the state of Oklahoma, Addison's intelligence and lineage were being questioned by a large man with no hair, sporting a tattoo of a pit bull on his right bicep.

"Were you born in a barn? Have you never made a bed? Didn't your parents teach you anything? This isn't rocket science, Gardner. Now do it again and do it right."

"No, sir, I was not born in a barn. Yes, sir, I have made a bed. Yes, sir, my parents taught me a great deal. Sir, I would be happy to remake my bed, sir. Thank you for giving me the opportunity to get it right, sir."

"And what kind of name is Addison anyway? That sounds like a girl's name."

Addison cursed his parents underneath his breath.

Addison Gardner had been in the army less than a week and was giving serious thought to renouncing his citizenship, fleeing the country to a banana republic, and seeking political asylum.

That very morning, in the midst of a pleasant dream about his mother's cooking, which he desperately missed, he had been wakened at two in the morning and made to walk ten miles in the rain carrying a sixty-pound rucksack. The bald man had been right beside him the entire way, pointing out his many shortcomings, prophesying his quick and gruesome demise should he ever encounter an enemy.

"I've got a little daughter at home who could kick your butt."

Addison didn't doubt it for a minute. His daughter probably looked just like him—bald and tattooed.

In his eighteen sheltered years, Addison had never met anyone like his sergeant. He had grown up in the comfortable confines of a minister's home, and had gone to church every Sunday; there he had been taught that Jesus loved him, and not just him, but everyone, including baby lambs, which Jesus carried on his shoulder, if the picture in the basement classroom of Harmony Friends Meeting could be believed. Now to meet the living, breathing personification of Satan, to come face-to-face with the Antichrist, the seven-headed beast of Revelation, was to realize Dale Hinshaw had been right after all, that evil did exist in the world and that he, Addison Gardner, was now trapped in its clutches.

After the hike, they had returned to the barracks and been given fifteen minutes to shower, shave, and clean their quarters, which apparently wasn't long enough, given the reaction of their sergeant, who ordered them to do push-ups, then clean the floor with Q-tips.

That night before falling asleep, Addison studied both his feet, hoping against hope they weren't covered in blisters, but instead cancerous lesions requiring amputation that would lead to his subsequent discharge from the United States Army. Unfortunately, each of his fellow soldiers was similarly afflicted, and Addison thought it unlikely they all had cancer.

He lay in bed thinking of his friends back in Harmony, who at that moment were likely at the town park sitting on their car hoods, or at the Dairy Queen. Most of them would be going away to college, which hadn't seemed all that appealing back in the winter when he'd decided to join the military, but now seemed a most pleasant prospect and one he wished he'd considered a bit more carefully. He thought about their house in Harmony, then remembered it wasn't theirs any longer, so he wondered about their new home, which he hadn't seen, and probably wouldn't live to see.

He'd written home every week, as ordered by his sergeant, to report he was doing fine, was making friends, and thoroughly enjoying himself. That, too, was ordered by his sergeant.

"You think your parents want to hear that you're tired and homesick and miss your mommy and wish you could come home? No, they don't, so don't tell them that. Tell them you're fine, meeting nice people, and having the time of your life. Or you'll do push-ups until your arms fall off."

Addison had written his last letter in code, using every third letter to say his life was in jeopardy, the food was terrible, and to meet him outside the gate with a getaway car, false ID, and a thousand dollars in unmarked bills. All to no avail. His parents wrote back to tell him how proud they were of him, how happy they were that all was well, and to keep in touch. One evening, certain he would be dead within the next few weeks, he wrote a will leaving everything to his brother, whom, to his great surprise, he missed with all his heart.

He hadn't told anyone his father was a minister, which he feared would seem unmanly. Instead, he invented an entire family out of whole cloth, including a father who was a special agent for the FBI, a mother who was a martial arts instructor, and a brother who lived in Wyoming and worked as a cowboy. While he was at it, he added a sister to his family, a cheerleader at Duke, who might come visit him any day now and bring her cheerleader friends. It was the last family member, the imaginary one, that elevated his status. He had clipped a picture from *Sports Illustrated*, with a cheerleader in the distant, fuzzy background, and had passed it around his platoon.

"That's my sister right there. Heather. She doesn't have a boyfriend. She says the football players are too immature, that she wants to date a real man. She might be here at graduation."

His popularity soared. Now he just needed an attractive young woman to attend his graduation, posing as his sister. Amanda Hodge, Ellis and Miriam's niece, had grown into quite a looker, and was the perfect age, but was probably too honest for such deception. It didn't much matter anyway; he'd be dead of blisters by the time graduation rolled around.

He had spent the last two years complaining about Harmony, how small and boring it was, how everyone was stupid, how he couldn't wait to leave and never come back. His father laughed and said he'd felt the same way when he was Addison's age, which was his father's response to every complaint. Addison didn't believe his father had ever been his age, that the pictures of him that age were phony. The boy in the pictures had hair, for instance, and was skinny, and looked nothing like his dad.

But now, a few weeks into basic training, he wasn't so sure. Now his parents seemed a little wiser, a bit more interesting than he had once thought, more competent. He felt bad for creating a whole new family when his old family had been perfectly fine, certainly better than most. They worked hard, paid their bills, volunteered at the Corn and Sausage Days, and helped their elderly parents. He hoped no one would ask his father about his work as a special agent for the FBI. He didn't want his parents to know he'd lied about them, that what they did, until now, had seemed insufficient to him.

He couldn't wait to see them. He'd give the army four years, see a bit of the world, then go back to Indiana and get his degree. Maybe move back to Harmony and become a guidance counselor at the high school and when kids complained about how boring and stupid everyone was, how they couldn't wait to leave town, he would nod and say, "I felt the same way when I was your age." Then he would tell them to do what they must, since some lessons couldn't be taught, only learned.

34

Though Sam's official starting date had not arrived, he and Barbara made their way across the parking lot to meeting for worship the next morning, greeted their fellow Friends, and took a seat in the middle row, near the center of the meeting room. A nice, moderate, central position, not leaning toward any extreme, favoring neither the right nor the left. One had to be careful about such things, after all.

Ruby Hopper led worship and Wilson Roberts brought the message, which turned out to be an autobiographical sketch of his life—his birth in the city, his brief service in the military before being discharged because of a medical condition involving an excessive pus discharge, which he discussed at length. He then expounded upon his entry into the plumbing business, beginning as a plumber's assistant, working his way up the chain of command, until he founded his own business selling plumbing fixtures across the Midwest, culminating in his induction into the Plumbers Hall of Fame in 1989.

At the conclusion of worship, Ruby Hopper stood, welcomed Sam and Barbara, mentioned Sam would be bringing his first message the following Sunday, then said, "Doreen Newby will also be giving a talk about quilting. Please be sure to invite your friends for what promises to be an exciting program. There will be a pitch-in dinner following meeting for worship, so bring extra food for any visitors we might have."

That seemed odd to Sam. A lecture on quilting? During church? As if Wilson Robert's plumbing story weren't unusual enough. He made a mental note to ask Ruby Hopper about that curious phenomenon.

Doreen Newby rose to her feet.

"I'll be focusing especially on the wedding ring and log cabin quilts," she said. "Describing the history of each, along with samples of both quilts."

Doreen's husband, Wayne, beamed.

"Doreen made her first quilt when she was seven years old," he announced to the congregation.

Several people clapped.

"We look forward to your presentation, friend," Ruby Hopper said.

And with that, meeting for worship was over. Most of the members gravitated toward Sam and Barbara. Several invitations for lunch were extended, then Norma Withers suggested they eat together at a nearby cafeteria, which suited everyone except Wanda and Leonard Fink, who excused themselves and went home to eat bologna sandwiches.

The conversation was lively, and the food tasty. Sam and Barbara lingered at the table with Ruby Hopper, while the others eventually took their leave.

"I'm curious about something," Sam said, "and wonder if you could shed a little light on it."

"I'd be happy to. What's on your mind?" Ruby asked.

"Wilson's talk today was interesting, but not something one might typically hear in a church. And you announced that Doreen Newby will be speaking next Sunday on quilts. I've never seen anything quite like that in a meeting for worship. What is the thinking behind these talks? If you don't mind my asking."

"We started it after our last pastor left. We all take turns speaking about any topic of interest. It's been quite fascinating. Did you know Wilson designed one of the first low-flow toilets?"

"Amazing," Sam said. "Truly astounding."

"Norma Withers brought her Hummel figurines to church one Sunday and talked about them. She has over fifty. She collects them. We've been looking forward to Doreen's quilt talk for some time. She was going to give it this past winter, but we had to cancel church that Sunday because the furnace quit."

"I'm sure it will be interesting," Sam said. "But now that the meeting has a pastor, do you think it's still necessary to have the members bring a message?"

"Well, the elders talked about that, but it's become our favorite thing to do. We have asked everyone to limit their talk to no more than a half hour. With you speaking fifteen minutes, that will leave us time for two songs and an offering."

"What about time for silence?" Sam asked. "That's an important part of Quaker worship."

"Most of us didn't grow up Quakers. We're not used to silence."

"I see," Sam said.

So much for hoping he had found a normal church.

"I'm sure the lectures are interesting," he said. "But perhaps we should schedule them for another time, maybe one evening a month, with a dinner. Do you think the congregation would like that?"

"I'm not sure. We really enjoy hearing them. I think you'll come to like them, if you give them a chance."

"It's not that I don't like them," Sam explained. "I just think when people come to church, they're looking for something more spiritual. I know plumbing fixtures are important, but they hardly seem an appropriate topic for meeting for worship."

"Oh, dear, this is going to upset people," Ruby said. "The Sunday after Doreen talks about quilts, her husband, Wayne, wants to show us slides of his model train collection. He's built a whole town in his basement, with trains coming and going. He even has a replica of the meetinghouse."

While Sam Gardner had never been fanatical about religion like some pastors were, he did consider himself a spiritual person. The prospect of sitting in church while its members lectured about plumbing fixtures, quilts, and model trains made him want to stick his head in an oven and crank up the gas.

"Maybe instead of doing that during worship, we could have a pitch-in dinner once a month and invite someone from the meeting to give a talk on various topics," Sam suggested.

Ruby Hopper thought for a moment, frowning. "We already have our monthly pie supper. But I suppose we could have another pitch-in, if you wanted."

"What's a pie supper?" Barbara asked. "I've never heard of that."

"Oh, they're lots of fun. Everyone bakes some kind of pie and brings it to share with the rest of us. We always have a chicken pot pie or a beef pot pie or maybe a shepherd's pie for the entrée, then various other pies for dessert. We've been doing it for years."

"Why don't we have the lectures during the pie supper?" Sam said.

"We've never done that before, but I suppose I could ask," Ruby said. "Of course, we'd have to check with the pie committee. If they don't agree, we might have to keep things the way they are."

"Why don't you talk with them," Sam suggested.

Later that day, while Sam was reflecting on the morning, it occurred to him he had placed the central act of Christian community in the hands of a pie committee.

"Whoever heard of giving a pie committee the authority to decide what we do during worship? What kind of place is this?" he said to Barbara.

"I wonder who the clerk of the pie committee is," Barbara said.

"I didn't think to ask."

Just that morning, Ruby Hopper had presented him with a thick folder of papers detailing the business of the meeting. He retrieved it from the kitchen table and began sorting through it, looking for a list of committee members.

"It says here Ellen Hadley is the clerk. Do you remember meeting her?" Sam asked.

"Ellen Hadley. Ellen Hadley. I don't remember an Ellen Hadley," Barbara said. "Why don't you call Ruby and see who she is."

Sam dialed her number.

"I was just getting ready to phone you," Ruby said. "I've spoken with the clerk of the pie committee and she wants the lectures to stay a part of worship."

"Would that be Ellen Hadley?"

"Yes."

"Who exactly is she?" Sam asked. "I don't believe I've met her."

"You haven't yet, I don't think. She doesn't come to church

anymore. She got her feelings hurt by our last pastor and stopped attending. We thought if we put her in charge of the pie committee, she'd maybe come back."

"So a woman who no longer attends our meeting heads up a pie committee, which apparently has the authority to tell us what we can and can't do during worship? Do I have that right?"

"When you put it like that, it doesn't sound right, does it? But we're hoping she'll start coming back to church."

"Perhaps we can discuss this matter at our next elders' meeting," Sam said.

"That's a good idea. Ellen will be there and we can talk with her then."

"Why would Ellen be there?"

"We made her an elder, too, hoping to keep her involved," Ruby said.

That night, Sam, Levi, and Barbara discussed the situation while eating dinner.

"I never thought I'd miss Dale Hinshaw," Sam said.

"Oh, honey, it's not that bad."

"This morning we listened to a message about plumbing fixtures. A woman who never comes to church serves as an elder and the clerk of a committee, a pie committee no less, and has taken it upon herself to oversee our worship and no one wants to cross her for fear she'll quit altogether. As much as I disliked Dale, at least he didn't stand up during worship and talk about toilets."

"They mean well," Barbara said. "Cut them some slack. You don't have to change everything at once. Let them do their lectures. In a little while they'll get tired of doing it, and then you can suggest some changes. If you push the issue, they'll resist the change. It's human nature."

"You end up with the weirdest churches," Levi noted. "I wonder why that is?"

Sam suspected it might have something to do with a personal deficiency, so he preferred not to think about it.

"It's times like this I wish I had a superintendent I could talk with," Sam said.

"You don't need a superintendent to keep you from doing something stupid," Barbara said. "You have me. Now relax. You haven't been here two days and you're already complaining."

Though she was a pacifist, sometimes it was all Barbara could do not to throttle Sam. She went for a walk instead, while Sam and Levi stayed home to watch 60 *Minutes*. It was her first foray into the neighborhood, which turned out to be quite charming and not at all what she thought neighborhoods in the city would be like. When Sam had first told her Hope Friends Meeting was in the city, she imagined dilapidated buildings, graffiti, gang wars, skinny thugs with droopy pants selling drugs, and getting mugged, if not outright killed.

Instead, the neighborhood was very pleasant, the houses modest in size but tidy, the yards nicely landscaped with flowers. Children were out on their bicycles; their parents seated on porch swings. Many of them greeted her as she walked past. Two blocks from their house was a corner market. Next door was a hardware store, and down from that an Italian restaurant. Across the street was a public library. A public library two blocks from home! Joy of joys!

A man who appeared to be in his sixties was sweeping the sidewalk in front of the restaurant. He greeted Barbara, then opened the door to his restaurant and invited her in. At least she thought he did. He had a heavy Italian accent and was hard to understand. The only person in Harmony with an accent was

Myron Farlow's brother, Vince, who had been conked in the head while splitting firewood and had talked funny ever since.

"Come in, come in. You have some wine with me." He guided Barbara through the door, seated her at a table near the window, poured her a glass of wine, then poured one for himself and sat down across from her.

"My wife, she no longer alive. So I share my wine with you," he said. "I am Bruno."

Barbara reached across the table to shake his hand.

"Hello, Bruno. I am Barbara," she said. "It's a pleasure to meet you."

This would never happen in Harmony. The minister's wife didn't sit in a window drinking wine with an unmarried man, not if she wanted to hold her head up in public, that is. She'd lived in the city less than forty-eight hours and was already hitting the sauce with a man she barely knew. She hoped no one from Hope Friends Meeting walked by while she was there, lest she become the topic of the next lecture.

Bruno hadn't let go of her hand.

"You're a very, how do you say, striking woman," he said.

O Lord, she prayed, *please do not let my son walk by here and see his wine-slurping mother holding hands with a total stranger.*

She'd only had two sips of wine, but when one is not accustomed to alcohol, that can be potent. Her vision was slightly blurred. What had she become? Is this what the city did to people? She glanced across the street at the library. It was probably full of dirty books about middle-aged, married women running off to Italy with unattached men. Oh, Lord, what had she become?

35

Barbara felt better the next morning. A little headachy, but not quite as disgusted with herself. She hadn't wanted to be rude, so had finished the bottle of wine with Bruno before excusing herself and walking home. No reason to feel guilty. He was old enough to be her father, after all. Over in Italy, fifteen-year-old boys were customarily married with two or three children. Weren't they? She thought so. She told Sam about Bruno to satisfy her conscience.

"I met the nicest man yesterday on my walk. A lot older than us. Probably around a hundred or so. He owns the restaurant next to the hardware store."

"There's a hardware store in the neighborhood?" Sam asked, then began to talk about nuts and bolts and all manner of fastening devices, promptly forgetting all about the man who had made a pass at his wife and tried to get her pickled.

"I'll have to go see that hardware store," he said. "But first I must organize my new office."

His old office at Harmony Friends Meeting had once been a boiler room and was musty and dark. But when Hank Withers had designed the Hope meetinghouse, he had outdone himself at the office. Two walls were mostly windows, looking out into the beech trees. The other two walls were bookshelves made of cherry and walnut. The desk was built-in, nestled in the corner where the windows met, looking outside. The windows were tinted. He could look out, but people couldn't look in, which gave him time to hide if someone he didn't want to talk with approached the meetinghouse. He whispered a prayer of thanksgiving for Hank Withers.

Sam unpacked his boxes of old sermons and arranged them on the bookshelves. He organized them by years in loose-leaf binders on the off chance he became famous and his alma mater wanted his sermons after he died. Nearly fifteen hundred sermons, only a few of which he remembered, none of which he wished to preach again. He changed his mind too often to give the same sermon twice. He knew ministers who'd written three years of sermons and kept repeating them. They were the same ministers who bought joke books and looked up sappy stories on the Internet to include in their sermons, and made it seem as if the events had happened to them. Usually a story about a kid with leprosy.

He stacked his funeral eulogies next to his sermons. From time to time, when he was depressed, he would reread certain of them and be cheered up. It was comforting to remember some people were dead and no longer annoying anyone. In some instances, Sam believed death was God's way of evening the score. Some people are the source of great suffering and finally God knocks them off in a spectacular fashion and everyone has to act sad, but after the funeral they go home and say to their spouse, "He sure had that coming." When Bob Miles Sr. had finally died after a long, hateful life, Sam's father had said, at the funeral within earshot of half a dozen people, "It's about time he bit the dust. Meanest man I ever knew." Sam read Bob Sr.'s eulogy once or twice a month, always with great pleasure.

After arranging his papers, he sharpened a dozen pencils and placed them in the tray drawer of his desk, opened a box of stationery, and placed it within reach of his chair. So far, the only furniture in the office was the desk and chair, but the meeting had told him to go buy a new couch and two chairs. At Harmony, his office had been filled with castoffs people had dragged in from their homes. Chairs with three legs, a recliner with worn-through fabric, a coffee table with water stains, moth-eaten rugs, and old lamps with frayed cords that threw off sparks, causing Sam to leap out of his three-legged chair and stomp out small fires. The recliner had belonged to Bob Miles Sr. It had been donated by Bob Jr. and smelled like a dead geezer, like someone who had died on a Friday and not been found until the next Monday, which had in fact been the case. Sam had a theory that Bob Sr.'s spirit had stayed behind and settled in the recliner. Nothing else could explain the stink.

A new couch and two chairs! He didn't have to run his choices past a committee or seek anyone's approval. No one had to okay his fabric selection or ask if it was on sale. He didn't have to listen to anyone talk about how this was no time to be buying furniture what with children starving in Africa.

"It's your office," Hank Withers had told him. "You pick out the furniture. What do we care what it looks like? You'll be the one staring at it all day."

Sam was starting to think he could listen to a lot of lectures on plumbing fixtures for this kind of freedom.

After organizing his office, he drove to the furniture store

Hank Withers had recommended, selected a couch, two matching easy chairs, and a coffee table, then arranged for delivery.

He ate a late lunch with Barbara. Tuna salad sandwiches. She'd spent the morning working on the house, arranging the kitchen and hanging up their clothing.

"Well, what do you think so far?" Sam asked.

"I can't believe this house. It's so pretty. Everything is so tasteful. I can see why Wanda Fink wants to keep it nice."

"Yeah, well, I still think she's a little kooky," Sam said.

"I'm almost embarrassed to put our furniture in here," Barbara said. "It smells like dirty socks."

"You can come over to my office and smell my furniture anytime you want," Sam offered. "Brand-new. Just picked it out."

Sam looked around the kitchen and into the living room. Their furniture did look a bit shabby.

"When we get a little money ahead, we can buy some new furniture," he promised.

It had taken him almost thirty years to get their furniture broken in and comfortable, but he was fairly certain they'd never get a little money ahead so went ahead and promised Barbara. The furniture had belonged to his grandmother. She had won it, an entire living room suite, on the *Gil Gillock Garden Hour*, after correctly spelling the word *chrysanthemum*. The prize didn't include delivery, so Ellis Hodge had driven her in his stock truck to Cartersburg, where she had visited Richard "Mother, Put the Coffee Pot On!" Bennett's Furniture Store, and selected a couch, two chairs, a coffee table, three lamps, two end tables, and a rubber plant. She was dead two weeks later, causing many people to wonder why God had let her win all that furniture only to knock her off before she'd even removed the plastic covers.

Sam and Barbara had lived on other people's furniture their entire married lives, except for their bed. Harvey and Eunice Muldock had offered them their old mattress and box spring when they'd moved to Harmony, but Barbara had refused to accept it.

"I am not going to sleep on the same mattress that Harvey Muldock's bare, bony butt has lain on the last twenty years. We'll buy a new mattress."

They had bought it on time, thirty dollars a month for thirty months. Nine hundred dollars for a mattress that formed a trough in the middle after six months. They woke up each morning, their backs throbbing, their necks stiff, their vertebrae locked in place. Sam calculated their mattress had shaved ten years off their lives.

"Maybe instead of getting a new couch, we can buy a new mattress when we get some money ahead," Barbara said that night, lying in the trough next to Sam.

"Maybe the meeting will grow so big, I'll get a raise and we can buy a new couch and a new mattress," Sam said, ever the dreamer.

"I need a new mattress, too," Levi called out from the next room. "This one smells like pee."

"When is he going back to Purdue?" Barbara whispered to Sam.

"I heard that," Levi said. "This Thursday."

"We love you, Son," Sam said. "Good night."

"Good night, Dad. Night, Mom."

Sam lay awake, cuddling next to his wife and feeling amorous, so he thought of Wanda Fink to tamp those feelings down. Thursday couldn't come soon enough.

36

~

What's that noise?" Barbara said, shaking Sam awake.

"What noise?"

"Listen."

Then Sam heard it. Music. A saxophone.

"Did you leave the radio on?" he asked.

"No. It's not the radio. It's coming from outside."

Sam threw the covers off and peered out the window.

"It's Hank Withers," he said.

"What in the world is Hank Withers doing outside at six in the morning?" Barbara asked.

"He appears to be sitting on the bench outside of the meeting-house playing a saxophone."

"Tell him to knock it off!" Levi yelled from his room. "I'm trying to sleep!"

Sam pulled on his pants and a shirt, ran a wet comb through his hair, then walked across the parking lot.

Hank lowered his saxophone.

"Morning, Sam. How are you this fine summer morning?"

"We're fine, thank you, Hank. What brings you out here so early in the morning."

"Reverberation," Hank said.

"Excuse me?"

"Reverberation. If I sit here and play my saxophone toward the meetinghouse I get the nicest reverberation. Didn't realize that when I designed it. Just got lucky, I guess. I like to come over here in the morning and play while the world's still quiet. Norma doesn't like me playing at home. Says it wakes her up."

"I can imagine it would," Sam said.

"Yeah, I don't mind playing outside. In fact, I've come to prefer it. Gets a little cold in the winter, though."

"You play here in the winter?"

"Every Tuesday, Thursday, and Saturday. Bright and early," Hank said. "You play an instrument, Sam? Maybe we could play together."

"No, no, I never learned to play an instrument. Took piano lessons when I was a kid, but it didn't pan out."

"That's a shame," Hank said. "I've found music to be very relaxing. Why, some mornings I'll sit and play for hours."

"Then I'll leave you to it," Sam said. "Enjoy your day."

He walked back to the house, poured a bowl of cereal, and was seated at the table when Barbara came in, coffee cup in hand, and sat across from him.

"Is this going to be a regular thing?" she asked.

"Tuesdays, Thursdays, and Saturdays," Sam said.

"Oh, Lord."

"He's actually pretty good. It might grow on us."

Their telephone rang.

"For crying out loud!" Levi yelled from his room. "Who is calling us at six fifteen in the morning?"

"Maybe it's the army," Barbara said, jumping up from the table and hurrying to the phone. "I hope Addison's all right."

She lifted the phone off the hook.

"Hello. Gardner residence."

"Good morning. It's Norma Withers. I'm looking for Hank. He wouldn't happen to be there, would he?"

"As a matter of fact he is. Would you like me to get him?"

"Oh, no. I don't want to bother you with that. Just tell him to bring home a gallon of milk from the store, if you could, please."

"Yes, I'll tell him."

"And some eggs and bread, too, please. And orange juice. And tell him he's almost out of MiraLAX, so if he wants some more, he should get some of those, too."

"Milk, eggs, bread, orange juice, and MiraLAX," Barbara repeated. "Got it."

"Tell him jumbo eggs, not large."

"Jumbo eggs, not large. Okay."

"Do you prefer jumbo eggs?" Norma Withers asked. "I've always liked the extra whites for cooking."

"I haven't given it much thought," Barbara said. "But I suppose you're right. I better go catch Hank, so I'll let you go."

"Thank you, dear."

Barbara conveyed the message to Hank, discussed the virtues of jumbo eggs, then came inside, ate breakfast, showered, and continued unpacking.

Sam went to his office at the meetinghouse, sneaking in the back door so Hank Withers, still wailing away on his saxophone, wouldn't see him. He had never realized how difficult it was to concentrate while listening to someone play a saxophone. What a racket! He turned on his radio to drown out the noise, then got out the meeting directory and began memorizing names. He was surprised to learn the meeting had more than one hundred and fifty members, most of whom, he observed, lived near the meetinghouse, though only a dozen of them attended with any regularity. How did a meeting of one hundred and fifty members have only twelve attenders?

Maybe Hank had played the saxophone during meeting for worship, he thought. *That would certainly explain the exodus. Or maybe there had been a big church fight, or a boring pastor.*

During the interview, they had made it seem as if people had died off or drifted away over the years. He looked at the date on the cover of the directory. Three years old. He wondered what had happened in the past three years. Had to have been a church fight. He wondered why they hadn't mentioned it to him. Maybe there were still raw feelings. He wished he could phone the superintendent and ask, but he suspected the superintendent would be of little help.

Perhaps Hank would tell him. He glanced out the window and noticed Hank walking toward his car, getting ready to leave. He opened the window.

"Hey, Hank. You got a minute?"

Hank turned toward Sam.

"Sure, let me put my horn up, and I'll be right in."

Sam met him on the front stoop of the meetinghouse, the directory in his hand. Hank sat beside him.

"Did something happen here a few years ago that upset some people in the meeting?"

Hank frowned, then fidgeted and looked uncomfortable.

"It's probably not my place to say. Perhaps you should ask Ruby. She was clerk of the meeting then."

That was curious.

"I'm sure she wouldn't mind if you told me," Sam said.

"I'd rather not discuss it. It's water under the bridge. No use dredging up bad feelings. Now we've got ourselves a new pastor, so let's move forward."

"If you don't want to talk about it, then you don't have to," Sam said, though being a nosy sort, he was desperate to find out what had happened.

The presence of buried secrets thrilled him to no end, like stumbling upon a treasure map, hidden in an attic. One hundred and fifty members down to twelve. Where had they gone? What had happened? Where should he dig? In moments like this, Sam forgot all about the long hours and low pay. It was enough to realize others knew something he didn't. Something delicious and scandalous. Something they didn't wish to divulge, which had always been his preferred topic of conversation. The forbidden fruit. The apple on the tree. The snake egging him on.

I could be happy here, he thought. *Happy, indeed.*

37

Sam and Barbara drove Levi back to Purdue on Thursday. He was living off campus this semester to save money. Nine guys in a three-bedroom apartment. A hundred dollars a month each, another twenty for utilities, each boy responsible for his own meals. Levi took three cases of Campbell's chicken noodle soup. Seventy-two cans of soup. Twenty-four days at three cans per day. Roughly three dollars a day to eat. Not bad. Not bad at all.

"All that sodium," Barbara said on the way home. "His blood pressure is going to shoot through the roof. It'll probably kill him." She began to cry, thinking of her firstborn lying in a casket, killed by soup.

"He'll be fine," Sam said. "He's young. He can take it. Besides, he likes chicken noodle soup."

Supper was quiet that night, with the boys gone. Barbara wasn't feeling especially romantic and swatted Sam away at bedtime. He was too distracted to mind, thinking about the meeting and what might have happened to it.

Since Monday morning, he'd been visiting members of the

congregation, even the Finks, hoping one of them would rat someone out. He hadn't come right out and asked anyone what had happened, but had dropped hints, all to no avail. Of the millions of churches in the world, he had stumbled upon the one church whose members didn't gossip. What rotten luck.

On Friday morning, he visited Wayne and Doreen Newby. Wayne took him to the basement to show him his train set. Wayne was a talker, a regular gasbag, who droned on about model trains. Sam stuck with him, slipping in a question now and then, hoping to catch him off guard so Wayne would spill the beans. He asked Wayne how long he and Doreen had belonged to the meeting, and when Wayne said twenty years, Sam feigned fascination and asked Wayne for a brief history of the meeting.

"Tell me the high points and low points," he said.

Wayne told him about the first pie supper, a high point, and serving on the limb committee, a low point. He told Sam about a former pastor who collected rocks and another who'd found a dozen four-leaf clovers at one time.

"That fella was something else. He could spot a four-leaf clover a mile away."

"Amazing," Sam said. "Simply amazing."

"But you asked for the low points," Wayne said.

"I've found that being open about our struggles can help us overcome them," Sam said piously.

"Well, I don't know if the others would agree, but the worst time in my memory was when we switched hymnals about four or five years ago. Personally, I was against it."

Sam's pulse quickened. This must have been it. He had known congregations to split over hymnals, to go at one another hammer and tongs over music to the Lord.

"Did anyone leave?" Sam asked.

Wayne thought for a moment.

"Not that I remember. Oh, I stayed away for a week, but then Doreen asked me to come back, so I did."

"Did anything else happen a few years ago?" Sam asked, exasperated.

"Oh my, yes, that was a dreadful time," Wayne said.

"I've sensed something very painful happened, but no one wants to talk about it."

"I think it's because, looking back, we're kind of embarrassed it ever happened. It was one of those things that didn't have to happen. One thing about it, though, we sure learned our lesson. It'll never happen again. Not in this church."

Sam was beside himself. "Would you mind telling me what happened?"

"I don't know that I'm the one to tell you. I'm not the clerk of the limb committee. Maybe you ought to ask Hank Withers."

"Hank told me to ask Ruby Hopper, that she was the clerk when it happened."

Wayne paused. "Well, that's true. She was the clerk of the meeting when it happened, but Hank was the clerk of the limb committee."

"What's the limb committee got to do with what happened?" Sam asked.

"It was the limb committee that dropped the ball," Wayne said. "But don't tell Hank I said so. He's kind of sensitive about it."

"What happened?"

"Well, there was this big limb that had broken off a tree and it was dangling over the meetinghouse. The meeting had asked the limb committee to take care of it before it broke off all the way and punched a hole in the meetinghouse roof. But the committee put it off and put it off and then one night a storm blew up and knocked the limb down and, sure enough, it punched a hole in the roof."

"That's it? A tree limb caused the meeting to lose over a hundred members?"

"I don't remember that we lost anybody. Oh, sure, a few people were upset with Hank for dillydallying, but no one said anything to him. And he fixed the damage himself. He's real handy with that kind of thing."

"Did it cause a church fight?"

"No, we all get along pretty good with one another."

"I'm glad to hear that," Sam said glumly.

Wayne launched into the history of model trains, while Sam looked for an opening to escape. Wayne wouldn't let him depart until Sam promised to return the following week to see Wayne's latest acquisition—a Lionel Lincoln Funeral Train.

"They brought Ol' Abe's body right through here, you know. Sunday, April thirtieth, eighteen hundred and sixty-five. It was raining to beat the band. My great-grandfather was there. He was just a kid. He used to tell me about it when I was little."

Wayne began to tear up, thinking of Abraham Lincoln being dead, as if he'd just gotten the news.

"One of the soldiers guarding the casket was smoking a cigar and he threw it to the ground and my great-grandfather picked it up. It got passed down to me. Want to see it?"

Before Sam could object, Wayne was rifling through a cabinet, retrieving a brown object which he showed to Sam.

"Grandpa dipped it in varnish, so it's held up pretty well."
Wayne studied it. "Just think, this very cigar was touched by

someone who touched Abraham Lincoln. Pretty amazing when you think about it. I bet I could get some real money for it. Truth is, I'm counting on it funding my retirement. Don't have any kids I can pass it down to. I thought I might take it to that fella on that pawnshop show on TV and have him tell me what it's worth. I bet they've never seen anything like this."

"That would be a safe bet," Sam agreed. "They probably don't see a lot of used cigars."

After a lengthy discussion of Abraham Lincoln, Sam took his leave.

He'd only visited three members that week, but was already exhausted; still, he determined to press on. He was certain the meeting's refusal to acknowledge its dark secret was the reason for its dwindling numbers. When he got home, he Googled the meeting to see if perhaps someone had been murdered in the meetinghouse. He found the meeting's website. It hadn't been updated since the late nineties. The pastor before last was still listed as the minister. Sam had a faint recollection of him. A large, doughy man named Fred who had a colon condition. He had given a lengthy talk about it one year at the annual pastors' retreat. Maybe Fred had exploded in the pulpit one Sunday. That would certainly explain the exodus.

That afternoon he wrote his sermon, his first at Hope, encouraging the congregation to bear one another's burdens and so fulfill the law of Christ. Galatians 6:2.

"Let there be no secrets among us," he wrote. "Let us share with one another those things that cause us pain, those matters we'd like to forget that still hurt us." Then he would ask the congregation to enter into silence, giving them the opportunity to stand, as the Spirit led them, to share their burdens.

Sam loved Galatians 6:2.

He read the sermon to Barbara that evening, just before bedtime.

"Nice try," she said. "But wouldn't it just be easier to ask Ruby what happened?"

"Ministry is about subtlety," he told her.

"I thought it was about honesty."

"Well, that, too, but only as a last resort."

With that settled, they went to sleep.

38

They had their first visitors on Sunday—Janet Woodrum from the Harmony Public Library, with her mother and father in tow.

"Surprise, surprise," Janet said when she saw Barbara. "I came home for the weekend and thought it would be fun to see you."

Barbara hugged her. "I'm so glad you did. I've missed you. How have you been?"

While Barbara and Janet visited, Sam welcomed Janet's parents. Two possible new attendees in a congregation of twelve. Sam did the math. Sixteen percent growth on his first Sunday. Not bad.

Having served as a local doctor, her father knew several of the members, and those he didn't, his wife, the local elementary school principal, did.

"This is a pleasant surprise," Janet's mother said. "I didn't think we'd know so many people here."

Sam had already forgotten their first names, so he was relieved when Ruby Hopper approached them and greeted them by their first names—Dan and Libby. Ruby Hopper, it turned out, volunteered in the school library once a week, reading to the children.

"Ruby, I forgot this is your church," Libby Woodrum said. "What a pleasure to see you." She turned toward her husband. "Dan, this is Ruby Hopper. Ruby, this is my husband Dan."

"I've heard a great deal about you," Ruby said, shaking his hand. "All good. It's an honor to have you both at meeting today."

"The honor is ours," Dan Woodrum said. "My wife has spoken of you many times over the years. I'm glad we've finally met."

He glanced around the meetinghouse. "What a lovely building. Of course, Janet and Libby came here for scouting, but I never had the pleasure. This is how a church ought to feel. Why, it feels like it grew out of the ground, as if God planted it here. Such peace and beauty."

Sam was delirious with joy. At Harmony Friends, visitors were accosted by Dale Hinshaw and harangued about their faith, which Dale generally found lacking. If Dale didn't reach the visitor first, Fern Hampton did, planting herself in the meetinghouse doorway, scowling, with arms crossed, not unlike a bouncer in a bar. But Ruby Hopper was a natural—welcoming without being overbearing and a whiz at names.

Since Dan Woodrum was a retired physician, Sam began telling him about the hernia operation he had undergone several years before, and how he had nearly died.

"I'm sure Dr. Woodrum doesn't want to hear about your hernia," Barbara said, taking Sam by the arm and guiding him to his spot on the facing bench. "Besides, it's time for meeting to start."

She whispered in his ear, "Don't blow it. I like it here."

The conversations died down as people took their places.

Barbara sat with the Woodrums, next to Janet, delighted her friend had come to visit. A few moments of silence passed, Sam rose to his feet, welcomed everyone, and expressed his joy at serving as their new pastor. They sang a hymn, one unfamiliar to Sam, about the interconnectedness of trees and whales and Native Americans. It was from a new Quaker hymnal Sam had heard about, but had never seen, on account of Dale Hinshaw declaring it liberal gobbledy-gook, the proceeds of which went to arm communist revolutionaries.

Norma Withers played the piano, quite well in fact, then Sam delivered what he believed to be his finest sermon ever. Thus he was surprised when no one stood to applaud at its conclusion. They sat silently, Sam wanting to give them ample opportunity to express their appreciation for his message, but apparently they were too deeply moved for words. So after a few moments Doreen Newby made her way forward to the pulpit, quilts in hand.

In the excitement of the morning Sam had forgotten that Doreen Newby was pumped and primed to gab about quilts for thirty minutes. Sam closed his eyes and bowed his head, as if in prayer, wondering how he might redeem the worship service so the Woodrums wouldn't think they were kooks with a quilt fetish. He begged God to strike Doreen with a sudden case of laryngitis, but God seemed in no hurry to answer his prayer and Doreen droned on, showing one quilt and then another. Sam was never going to build a church this way.

Eventually, after what seemed like days, Doreen finished. They sang another song, this one about God being a mother. Sam offered a closing prayer, then people turned to the person next to them and shook hands.

Dan Woodrum was the first to reach him.

"That was the most profound message I've ever heard in a church. Simple, touching, insightful."

"Thank you," Sam said, trying his best to appear modest.

"I'll admit," Dan went on, "when I saw her come forward with her quilts, I had misgivings, but when she began talking about her grandmother making them during the Depression from scraps of cloth to keep the children warm, I remember my grandmother doing the same. What a timely reminder of human compassion."

A tear leaked from his eyes.

"Forgive me, I haven't been moved like this in years. Then we sang that song about the feminine qualities of God. It all fit together so beautifully."

He pulled a handkerchief from his pocket and blew his nose.

"It's a little program we began sometime ago. We ask someone each week to speak on a topic dear to their heart," Sam said.

"Well, it's brilliant. I must admit, and please don't take offense, but I have grown weary of pastors going on and on every Sunday. God can speak through others, as we clearly saw this morning."

"That was my thinking, too," said Sam, now taking full credit for a practice he'd spent much of the previous week trying to eliminate.

But Dan Woodrum didn't hear him. He was thanking Doreen Newby, and hugging her. Hugging her! As if she were his long-lost sister.

The men began setting up tables while the women hurried to the kitchen to bring out food.

Sam made his way to Janet and Libby Woodrum.

"I hope you'll join us for lunch," Sam said. "We have more than enough food."

"Barbara has already invited us, and we're planning on staying," Janet said. "Thank you for your message, Sam. It was nice."

Nice. Sam had learned long ago that when someone told him his sermon was nice, they hadn't been paying attention. Hitler could come back from the dead, stand in a church, announce the invasion of France, and every third person would pat him on the back and thank him for his nice message.

The food made up for it. Pies everywhere. And bless Doreen Newby's wacky heart, fried chicken, her grandmother's recipe. Sam sat beside Wilson Roberts, who regaled him with stories of Hope in the old days, before the city grew out to it.

"Yeah, when I was a kid, this was considered the country. The meetinghouse property was a cow pasture. Of course, the hardware store's right where it's always been. Have you been there yet?"

"Not yet. Hope to very soon, though."

"Man who runs that is named Charley Riggle. His family's been here ever since anyone can remember. Salt of the earth. Has a really nice plumbing section for such a small store."

"Just a bit past the hardware store is our grocery," Wilson continued. "The Droogers own it. They moved down here from Minnesota a few years ago. Good folks, but they talk kinda funny. You can tell they're not from around here. Maybe you and Barbara could shop there. We've been trying to get them to join the meeting. They've come once or twice."

Wilson Roberts was wound tighter than a tick. Sam was desperate to escape his clutches and woo the Woodrums, maybe wring out of them a promise to return. Visitors had to be finessed. The bait had to be dangled in front of them, the hook set, the line reeled in slowly. Next thing you knew, you had them landed in the boat, joining the church, and teaching a Sunday school class. There was an art to it.

He wondered if the Woodrums were tithers. Janet had once mentioned they belonged to a church. Sam wondered which one. He hoped it wasn't a liberal one. He liked liberals, but they were lousy givers. He preferred recovering conservatives with an expanding view of God but still afraid not to tithe. It was a fine line. You had to keep folks just a little afraid, or they wouldn't give a dime. Once they started talking about their brother the wolf and the Great Spirit, they were pretty well useless as far as tithing was concerned.

He caught up with the Woodrums as they were leaving. He thanked them for visiting, and invited them to return. They had stayed to clean up, which was a good sign. He was a bit too eager, following them out the door, when Barbara took his hand and squeezed it, hard. He watched as they walked to their car and drove away.

"Geez, Sam, I thought you were going to run out there and wash their car or something. Give them a little space," Barbara said.

"I just wanted them to feel welcome."

"Welcome is one thing, stalking is another. Try and relax. The world won't end if they don't come back."

Sam panicked. "Did they say they wouldn't come back?"

"No, now settle down. They said they enjoyed themselves and would be back."

"Those were their exact words?" Sam asked. "They said they'd be back?"

"Yes, those were their exact words. Now go back inside and be with the others."

While Barbara stood outside on the meetinghouse porch, Sam went inside and helped put away the tables, still wondering what in the world a Quaker meeting could have done to take upwards of a hundred and fifty members down to twelve.

39

"Maybe they killed them and buried them underneath the meetinghouse," Barbara said that night to Sam, while they were lying in bed.

"It's built on a slab," Sam pointed out. "That would have been next to impossible. Besides, I don't think Ruby Hopper is the killin' type."

"She is sweet, isn't she? Did I tell you she sent a pie home with me? Chocolate cream."

"I love that woman," Sam said.

"For a group that likes to eat so much, I'm surprised they don't have a bigger kitchen with a fellowship hall."

"I talked to Hank Withers about that. He said he designed the meetinghouse with those things in it, but the meeting didn't have enough money when they built, so they made the kitchen smaller and left off the fellowship hall altogether."

"Wouldn't it be nice if we could add those someday?" Barbara said.

"It'll take a lot more than twelve members to pull that one off," Sam said.

"I hope the Woodrums come back," she said.

"I thought you told me they said they were going to."

"They said they would, but everyone says that."

"They seemed to enjoy themselves," Sam said. "They really liked Doreen's quilt talk."

"Who's talking next Sunday?"

"Wayne is talking about his model train collection," Sam said. "That ought to pack 'em in."

With Levi back in college, Sam had been anticipating an evening of romance, but now he was preoccupied, worrying how the Woodrums felt about model trains. Maybe Dan Woodrum had a train set as a child and would break down in tears remembering it and write the meeting a check for ten thousand dollars.

Then Sam began wondering, while lying in bed, when he had started stewing about the church's finances. It was a side of him he didn't like, his calculating side, his side that worried, causing him to defer to the wealthier people in his congregation, hoping to stay in their good graces. At Harmony, he'd never given money much thought, probably because the Peacocks had won the lottery and once a month threw in a check big enough to choke a horse. He sensed money was an issue at Hope Meeting, notwithstanding the wealth of Wilson Roberts's toilet empire. Sam wanted to value everyone, whether they gave much or little. He thought about this at such length that when he turned toward Barbara she was sound asleep, caring not one whit for his manly needs.

They had hoped to sleep in the next morning, their day off, but at six thirty they awoke to the sound of a saxophone.

"I thought he only played on Tuesdays, Thursdays, and Saturdays," Barbara said.

"That's what he told me last week."

Sam climbed out of bed, closed their bedroom windows, and went back to bed.

"I can still hear him," Barbara said.

"You know, he's not that bad. I've always liked that song. What's it called?"

"'Moon River.'"

"Ah, yes. Now I remember. We had it played at our wedding, didn't we?"

"We sure did," Barbara said, scooting closer to him, nuzzling his neck.

Sam loved a good neck nuzzle as much as the next man.

What happened next caused him to wish Hank Withers came over every morning to play his saxophone.

Afterward, they went for breakfast at a coffee shop in their neighborhood. Past the hardware store, past the Italian restaurant where Bruno had tried to seduce Barbara, past the library and Drooger's Food Center, then around the corner to the coffee shop for bagels and coffee grown at a Lutheran commune in Argentina by the descendants of Nazis who had fled there after World War II.

"It says here that ten percent of the money they make goes to Jewish charities," Barbara said, reading her cup.

"Boy, everyone's selling coffee these days. Now the Nazis are in on it."

"They're not Nazis. Their parents and grandparents were. They're trying to make up for it. I think it's nice."

Sam, who had never been much of a coffee drinker, said he would stick with hot chocolate, whose beans were picked by humble Christians in the Ivory Coast and Ghana.

They bickered for a while about the relative merits of coffee and chocolate, then went to the hardware store, where they purchased a mop and bucket.

"Gonna do some cleaning, eh?" the owner asked.

"I am," Barbara said. "He probably won't help much."

"You new to the area? Haven't seen you before."

"Yes," Sam said. "I'm the new pastor of Hope Friends Meeting. Name's Sam Gardner. This is my wife, Barbara."

"Pleased to meet both of you. I'm Charley Riggle. Call me Charley."

"You wouldn't happen to know Uly Grant, would you?" Sam asked.

Sam was under the impression all hardware store owners knew one another.

"No, can't say as I do. Should I?"

"He owns the hardware store in Harmony. That's where we're from. You're sure you don't know him? About six feet tall. A hundred and seventy-five pounds. Brown hair, mustache, beard. I bet you'd know him if you saw him."

"Maybe I'll have the pleasure one day," Charley Riggle said. "I've always found hardware store owners to be fascinating people."

They discussed sandpaper for a brief time, then Sam invited Charley to visit Hope Friends.

"You'd probably know quite a few people there," Sam said.

"Oh, I know just about everyone who goes there."

"Well, you're always welcome to join us."

"Thanks, I appreciate it."

They shook hands good-bye, then Barbara returned to the parsonage to continue organizing, while Sam headed to his office. He'd made his way halfway through the directory memorizing names. He was up to the P's, of which there were several.

No Q's. That didn't surprise him. Q's were hard to come by. He'd had a Q in his first church, a Quinett, but never one since.

He began studying the R's. There were three Rawlses. He hadn't met them yet. He looked up their address on Google Maps. They lived less than a mile from the meetinghouse. He wondered why they no longer attended.

His eyes skipped down the list to Riggle. Riggle. Hmm, where had he heard that name? He wished he was better at remembering names. He closed his eyes in thought, and was soon asleep, waking just in time for lunch.

40

Libby Woodrum was having a dreadful day. Two teachers had phoned to announce their retirement, giving her less than a week to find replacements, then the school librarian had quit in a huff. Days like this made Libby wonder why she had ever wanted to be a school principal. The flower beds lining the front sidewalk were choked with weeds; she had asked the head custodian a week ago to hoe them, but nothing had been done. She had found him the day before napping in his workshop. It would take an act of Congress to fire him. Some things were just easier to do herself.

She picked up her phone and dialed her daughter, Janet, in Harmony, who answered on the third ring.

"Hi, Mom."

"Hi, honey. Sorry to bother you at work, but I need some help. I've lost my librarian and was wondering if you knew anyone who graduated with you who might still be looking for work."

"Don't you have to post the job opening within the school system first?" Janet asked.

"Ideally, yes. But I checked with personnel and only two people have degrees in library science and they don't want to transfer. So I can go outside the corporation, and I was hoping you might know someone who would do a good job."

"To be honest, I haven't been keeping up with everyone else. Would you like me to e-mail the university's placement department to see if anyone is looking for a job?"

"That would be wonderful," said Libby Woodrum. "Give them my contact information, if you don't mind."

"Will do, Mom."

"You're a wonderful daughter."

"Yes, I am, aren't I."

Just as Libby was hanging up, Janet said. "Hold on, Mom. You know, Barbara Gardner has a degree in library science. And she's a whiz with kids. You ought to see if she might be interested."

"Well now, there's a thought. She seemed sharp."

"She is. No drama, either. You won't have to hold her hand."

"My kind of gal. You wouldn't happen to have her phone number, would you?"

Janet passed along Barbara's number and they talked a bit longer. Libby began to pry, asking whether Janet and Matt the Unitarian minister were serious, and whether there might be a wedding down the road and possibly grandchildren they could spoil.

No, no, and no. In fact, Janet told her, she thought she might be a lesbian and would likely never marry or have children, which wasn't true, but it silenced her mother.

Libby phoned the parsonage, but no one answered, so she left her name and number. She spent the rest of the day looking for teachers, most all of whom had already found jobs teaching elsewhere, except for one recent college graduate who said *like* and *you know* five times a sentence. She crossed his name off the list.

When she left for the day, she found Hank and Norma Withers weeding the flower beds by the school entrance.

"Bless your hearts," she said. "But you don't have to do this."

"Probably wouldn't do it if we had to," Hank said. "When we brought our grandson here the other day to get registered, we noticed the flower beds needed a little attention. I imagine the janitors are busy getting the inside ready."

"It's very kind of you," Libby Woodrum said. "We appreciate it."

"I'll come back tomorrow, spread some mulch, and you'll be in fine shape," he said. "I might even put up a couple of bird feeders, so the kids can watch the birds."

"You are absolute saints," Libby Woodrum said, hugging them.

She walked the four blocks thinking well of Quakers. A bit odd, perhaps, talking about quilts during worship, but civic-minded. She wondered if Hank or Norma had a teacher's certificate. That would be interesting. Bring in a senior citizen to whip the place into shape. Hmm.

Sam was the first to discover the telephone message from Libby Woodrum.

"I wonder what she wants," he said to Barbara. "Maybe she's calling to talk about my sermon."

Sam had long harbored the fantasy that people meditated upon his sermons for days after he'd given them.

"I'm sure that's it," Barbara said. "What else could she want?"

Sam dialed the Woodrums' number. Libby answered the phone and they exchanged greetings.

"It was certainly nice having you with us this past Sunday," Sam said, deftly sliding into the topic of church.

"Yes, well, we had a very nice time," she said. "We've been having a difficult time in our church lately, so it was nice to go to church and just enjoy it."

They were on delicate ground. Sam wanted to appear sympathetic, but not overeager.

"For all its blessings, community can be difficult at times," he said. "And while change is often helpful, it's never easy."

Smooth. Sometimes he amazed himself.

"Is Barbara home this evening?"

Sam handed the phone to Barbara, then hovered nearby as she greeted Libby. He couldn't make out the conversation, but his wife seemed pleased.

"Oh, I'd be happy to come talk with you about that. What time would you like to meet? Ten o'clock tomorrow. That's perfect. I'll see you then."

She hung up.

"Talk about what?" Sam asked. "Talk about the church? What's she want to know? Did they like it?"

"No, she doesn't want to talk about the church. She wants to talk about a librarian job at her school."

"Oh."

"Oh? I get a possible job offer and that's all you can say? No 'Congratulations'? No 'Wow, that's great'? No 'I'm happy for you'?"

"Of course I'm happy for you. You know that."

"If she had phoned to compliment you on your sermon, you'd be dancing a jig," Barbara said. "But I get good news and you just say, 'Oh.' Sam Gardner, sometimes I could just shake the snot out of you."

"Absolutely uncalled for," Sam said. "I'm terribly sorry. Why don't I take you out for dinner to make up for it? Let's go to that Italian place next to the hardware store. What's it called? Bruno's, is that it?"

"I've heard the food is bad," Barbara said, slightly panicked. She had heard of jilted Italians losing their temper and killing people. Though Sam annoyed her, she had no wish to see him dead.

"Really? Wilson Roberts said it was delicious. So did Ruby Hopper. Come on, let's give it a try."

Sam's presence had no apparent effect on Bruno. He greeted Barbara with a kiss on both cheeks, held her hand all the way to their table, told her she was lovely, and said if she ever ditched Sam, he would be happy to marry her.

Barbara laughed. "Oh, I'll probably keep him."

"Well, you know, accidents happen," he said, smiling at Sam. He had pointy teeth, like a vampire. "Maybe if something happens to him, you might think of me."

He returned to the kitchen.

"Did he just threaten to kill me?" Sam asked.

"Of course not. Stop being paranoid. He's a harmless old man."

The food was delicious, though Sam only nibbled at his, unable to simultaneously enjoy his dinner and keep a watch out for Bruno.

"I am very happy for you," Sam told Barbara over dessert. "I hope you get the job."

"I need to find out more about it, but it sounds perfect. Summers off. Two weeks at Christmas. Maybe the meeting could give you some extra time off in the summer and we could travel a bit."

They discussed other possibilities, then paid their bill. Sam left Bruno a generous tip, hoping to pacify him.

The sun was setting as they left the restaurant, and the day was cooling off, so they looped through the neighborhood. It felt a bit like Harmony, with old houses, shade trees, and people out puttering in their yards.

"Wilson Roberts said this was a little town and the city grew out to it," Sam observed.

"Yes, that's what Janet told me as well. The Woodrums go way back here."

"It's kind of neat," Sam said. "Feels like a small town, but we're twenty minutes from the center of the city."

"I think we're going to be happy here," Barbara said.

"I think so, too."

And as Sam said that, he meant it. He thought he would pine for his hometown, but so far he hadn't. He missed some of the people, Uly Grant and Miriam Hodge, but the lure of nostalgia had faded. He had been ready for something new, something different. Hope Meeting was certainly those things.

They turned down the meetinghouse lane, lined with pine trees on one side and apple trees on the other. The apple trees sagged with ripening fruit.

"I love everything about this place," Barbara said.

"Yeah, I don't understand why more people don't come here. Something happened, but no one wants to talk about it."

"Oh, you'll find out in time. But for now, just get to know the folks, and let them get to know you."

It was good advice, which Sam decided to follow, at least until his curiosity got the best of him.

41

The next morning found Sam at the hardware store, purchasing lightbulbs he could have bought two dollars cheaper at Home Depot. But Charley Riggle didn't work at Home Depot, and Sam was hoping to snag Charley for the church.

"Thank you for the business," Charley said, as he placed the lightbulbs in a paper sack.

"Always happy to support my local hardware store," Sam said, then paused. "I don't know if you have a church home, but if you're interested, we would be honored if you visited our Quaker meeting."

"You don't know about me, do you?" Charley Riggle asked.

"What do you mean?"

"I was a member of the meeting up until three years ago, when they gave me the heave-ho."

"Gave you the heave-ho?" Sam asked, puzzled. "Why did they do that?"

Charley laughed. "Probably because I hadn't attended in years. Lost interest. I don't blame them for taking me off the membership rolls."

"I'm sorry about that. I didn't know."

"No need to apologize. The meeting has a right to have standards of membership."

"You're still welcome anytime," Sam said.

"I know. And I might come by some Sunday. I like the folks there. It's just that Sunday is my only day off and I like sleeping in, truth be told."

"I understand," Sam said.

"Hope you'll still do business with me now that you know I'm a heathen," Charley said, chuckling.

Sam reached across the counter and shook Charley's hand. "Some of my best friends are heathens."

Well, that certainly explained it, Sam thought, as he walked home. That's how you went from one hundred and fifty members down to twelve attenders. Boot 'em out. He wondered whose bright idea that had been. It sounded like something Dale Hinshaw would have done. Culling the weeds. Separating the sheep and the goats. Casting the sinners into utter darkness.

When Sam reached the meetinghouse, Hank Withers was there with his saxophone.

"Morning, Hank. Got a minute?" Sam asked.

"Sure."

They entered Sam's office and sat on the new couch.

"I've been reading the old membership directories and noticed we used to have a lot more members. Then something happened and now we don't. No one wants to talk about it. But I was just at Charley Riggle's hardware store and he told me the church threw him out. Would you mind telling me what happened?"

"Oh boy, here we go again," Hank said. "I'd rather not revisit this issue, Sam. Things are finally settling down."

"I'm not going to stir things up. I just want to know what happened. It's like not telling your doctor about the time you had cancer. If I'm going to be your pastor, I need to know the meeting's history."

Hank thought for a moment, then sighed. "I suppose you're right. Three years ago, we fired a hundred and thirty-two members."

"Fired? How can you fire a church member?"

"Well, it wasn't easy, but we did it. These were folks who no longer darkened our doorstep, who never did any kind of ministry with us, never showed any interest, and never helped. We hadn't heard from most of them in over ten years. But every year, we had to send the yearly meeting office over twenty thousand dollars because they were on our rolls. Four years ago, we didn't have the money, so didn't send it in. We can't send what we don't have. The superintendent came and read us the riot act. He hadn't been here in years, but when we stopped paying our full assessments he was here the next week.

"So," Hank continued, "we decided to update our membership rolls. We sent notices to folks explaining the problem, inviting them back, but no one came back. Only a few bothered to get in touch with us. If someone was too old or worked on Sunday, we urged them to be active in other ways. If they agreed to, we kept them on; if they didn't, we let them go. We're down to twenty members now. Twelve of us are active, and eight are too old or sick to participate any longer, but they're part of our prayer life and we visit with them regularly."

"So what happened then?" Sam asked.

"It caused the biggest mess you ever saw. We got the nastiest letters. We'd see some of them out in public and they'd tear into us. Poor Ruby Hopper, she was our clerk then, and her phone rang off the hook. She can hardly talk about it today without crying."

"Is that why the superintendent has been ignoring you?"

"Yes, he says we owe the yearly meeting twenty thousand dollars, and that until we pay we're not in good standing."

"You lost your pastor right around then, didn't you?" Sam asked.

"Yes, he said he wouldn't work at a meeting that didn't pay its assessments. But right after that, the superintendent got him a bigger meeting, then told us he wouldn't help us find a new pastor."

"Well, that explains some things," Sam said. "Like why it took the meeting three years to find a new pastor."

"Yeah, no one wanted to interview with us without the superintendent's blessing. We had to go around him to get you, and even then he told us not to hire you."

When Sam had first become a pastor, he'd believed in hell. Then he'd pretty well decided it didn't exist. But whenever he thought of the superintendent he was inclined to believe in it and suspected the superintendent would one day run it.

"Well, that's the church at its worst," Sam said. "I hear things like that and it makes me want to find a new line of work."

"It was awfully discouraging," Hank said.

They sat quietly in the office, thinking.

"You know," Sam said, "there may only be twelve people in this meeting, now fourteen counting Barbara and me, but I think we have a lot going for us."

"I just don't understand why we haven't grown," Hank said. "We invite people and they'll come for a Sunday or two, but don't come back."

"It's kind of tricky," Sam said. "When there are so few people in a congregation, new people can't help but feel they're not part of the group. It's kind of like being invited to a family dinner when you're the only guest. Everyone else seems to belong except for you."

"That's a good analogy," Hank said. "I never thought of it that way."

"So we just have to figure out a way to help people feel part of our family right off the bat."

They contemplated that for a moment.

"If you don't mind, I am going to return to my saxophone," Hank said. "It helps me think."

"You do that, and I'll tend to my work."

Sam had been hoping for more drama. He'd spent the past several weeks wondering what calamitous event could have spurred such an exodus from the meeting—a doctrinal disagreement, a grab for power, a dispute over carpet color. But no, they'd dumped 132 church members to save money. Just once he'd like to see a church lose members over something worthwhile, maybe have a good fight over a significant matter, such as a minister performing a same-gender marriage, for instance.

He wondered, not for the first time, if he had left Harmony Meeting too soon. He'd told Miriam Hodge he'd wanted to avoid a congregational fight, but there were worse things. Silence in the midst of injustice being one. Maybe he should have stayed and gone head-to-head with Dale Hinshaw, and let the congregation decide which direction to go, rather than let Dale lead them around by the nose. But no, he quit to avoid a fight, when a fight might have been the best thing. He wondered if it was too late to get his old job back.

42

The school was an old one, built in 1929, according to the date carved in stone over the front entrance. Barbara thought it looked like a temple to education, a church of enlightenment. Though it was only five blocks from their home, she and Sam hadn't yet noticed it in their evening walks. Libby Woodrum was seated on a bench underneath a tree awaiting her arrival.

"What a beautiful building," Barbara said, by way of greeting.

"One of the oldest elementary schools in continuous use in the state," Libby said. "Big and drafty, but abounding with good spirits, including one ghost, or so our janitor claims."

"Ooh, a ghost! I hope it's a nice one."

"A bit less intense than when she was alive. It's Mrs. Helton. She taught here nearly fifty years. She approached education like war, a one-woman campaign against sloth and ignorance. When she retired, we said this place wouldn't be the same without her. So when she died, she apparently decided to return. Our janitor sees her at night, in the teachers' lounge, grading papers."

"Well, at least she's keeping busy," Barbara said. "Nothing worse than a ghost with time on its hands."

"Yes, they stir up all kinds of trouble, don't they!"

They made their way inside to Libby's office.

"I would like you to be our new librarian," Libby Woodrum said. "It won't be easy. Our former librarian did not distinguish herself, so now I have five hundred children who are scared to death of books."

"I would love to be your new librarian, but shouldn't you interview me first?"

"I did better than that. I asked my daughter Janet about you. She thinks you'd make a fantastic school librarian. Her endorsement is good enough for me."

"When did you want me to start?"

Libby glanced at her watch. "How about in five minutes?"

"I can do that."

"I'll get the paperwork going, but right now I'll give you a tour of the school and introduce you to the teachers. I can't tell you how much I appreciate this, Barbara. The library has long been a concern of mine, and I think with you in there, we can turn it around."

"Thank you for your confidence in me," Barbara said. "I will do my absolute best."

She excused herself to phone Sam and tell him the good news, then walked with Libby through the school, meeting the teachers and staff, who were delighted to meet her, which made her think the previous librarian had been a terror.

The library was stately, high-ceilinged, but had not been well tended. Books were stacked haphazardly on the shelves, dust had accumulated in the corners, and a musty odor permeated the place. Judging by the stale air, the windows hadn't been opened in years.

It took her a half hour to wrestle the windows open. She lubricated the sashes with a bar of soap she carried in her purse, being the mother of two sons, and within a short time had the windows gliding smoothly up and down. Fresh air did wonders for the place. She made her way to the basement for a can of Pledge and a box of dust rags, which the custodian seemed reluctant to hand over until she pointed out that he was free to dust the library if he wished.

"And I'll need a clean mop and a bucket of hot water with Murphy's Oil Soap," she said. "And a dust mop. Don't forget a dust mop."

The children would be arriving in two weeks, and she was going to be ready for them, come hell or high water.

She worked through the day, then left for home, where she found Sam lying on the couch, a heating pad on his forehead, brooding.

"I think I made a mistake," he said. "I called Miriam Hodge this afternoon and they're going to let Paul Fletcher go. They want me back. Even Bea and Opal Majors said they might have acted too hastily. I was wrong to leave. I wanted to avoid a church fight over homosexuality, but now I think we should have faced the topic head-on. They're going to have to deal with it sooner or later. I was wrong to leave. I should go back."

"When did you decide all this?" Barbara asked. "Because when you left this morning, you were headed to a hardware store in a wonderful mood, glad to be here."

"I found out why they lost all those members," Sam said. "Hank Withers told me."

"Why?"

"They wanted to save money so they kicked out their inactive members so they wouldn't have to pay an assessment on them."

"Well, that makes sense. They're a small church; they don't have the money to pay for a bunch of deadbeats cluttering up the church rolls. At least they did something. Heck, Harmony wouldn't take people off the church rolls even after they'd died. Don't you remember that? We kept Fern Hampton's mother on the rolls for five years because Fern threw a fit when we pointed out her mother could no longer be a member since she was dead. Now you have a church with the guts to toss out the loafers and you get melancholy and want to go home."

"I think I might have acted too hastily, that's all."

"I knew this would happen," Barbara said.

"You knew what would happen?"

"I knew once you got away from there, you would start finding reasons to go back. That town has a grip on you. When you're there, you complain about how it drives you crazy, but when you're not living there, you want to move back. I don't know what to do with you, Sam Gardner."

"I want to move back."

"I'm staying here."

"You can't be serious," Sam said. "You wouldn't go with me?"

"Sam, I have followed you around all our married life. We went to Illinois to a church that didn't work out. Then we moved to your hometown. I've been caring for our sons all this time, and never had the chance to do what I went to college to do. When I got a job in Harmony, I had to leave it. Now I have a job here, and you're asking me to quit. I'm not going to do it."

"This church only has twelve people. How we can make it here?"

"You knew that from the start, but you accepted the job anyway. Now stop moping, get off your butt, and get busy pastoring."

"I don't have the energy to start all over."

"You'd better find the energy. These people are depending on you and you promised them you could help them. Now get off the couch, take a shower, and put on some clean clothes. We've been invited out to eat with the Woodrums. Hank and Norma are coming, too."

Sam jumped up from the couch. "The Woodrums? Did you invite them or did they invite us?"

"They invited us. Apparently, Hank and Norma cleaned the flower beds at school and Libby wanted to take them to dinner as a thank-you. We've been invited along."

"Well, that's a good sign," Sam said, momentarily forgetting his fatigue. "What should I wear?"

"Khakis and a dress shirt. We're going to Bruno's."

"The guy who wants to kill me?"

"That's the one."

Sam plugged in the iron and began pressing his shirt.

"I bet the Woodrums will end up joining the meeting," he said. "Wouldn't that be great?"

"Yes, I do like my new job," Barbara said. "Thank you for asking."

"What do you mean? I didn't ask."

"My point exactly. It would have been nice if you had," Barbara said.

"Oh, I get it. How did your new job go today?"

"It was wonderful, I—"

"Where's the starch?" Sam yelled.

"—think it's going to be a wonderful experience."

"Well, that's great, honey. I'm proud of you. Say, do you think if the Woodrums join the meeting, they could maybe bring in some people from their old church? If the Woodrums are unhappy, there might be others wanting to change churches, too."

You can tell men wrote the laws, Barbara thought. *If women had written them, a wife would be forgiven the murder of her husband. Not just forgiven, but understood and sympathized with.*

"There, there," the judge would say at her trial, *"don't be too hard on yourself. He had it coming."*

43

We certainly appreciate you being able to join us on such short notice," Dan Woodrum said, after Bruno had seated them at a round table in the back corner of his restaurant.

"This evening is to thank Hank and Norma for their work on the school flower beds," said Libby. "We certainly appreciate it. And to welcome Barbara as the new librarian of Hope Elementary!"

Bruno brought a basket of warm bread to the table and handed it to Sam, who passed it around the table and watched as the others ate it and lived before helping himself to a piece. A bottle of wine was opened, glasses filled, and a toast offered to Barbara with wishes for her success.

"You'll be interested to know we took a test on the Internet, twenty questions to help us discern which denomination we should join, and it indicated we were liberal Quakers," Dan said.

"Well, what do you know about that!" Sam said, starting to quiver with excitement. "I guess this means you'll be joining the meeting."

Barbara kicked him under the table.

"Not that you have to," Sam added. "I just thought you might be considering it."

"Why don't you just come to meeting for worship," Hank Withers suggested. "If you become members, we'll have to pay an assessment on you each year."

The Woodrums had only attended meeting for worship once and Hank Withers was already trying to talk them out of joining.

"Joining might be premature, but we do think we'll start attending," Libby said. "To be honest, we're disgruntled with our church. It has not been a kind place for gay people. Sam, when Janet told us you had conducted a same-gender marriage in Harmony, we were impressed. It was a very brave thing to do."

"Marriage equality is something I believe in," Sam said. "I had given it a lot of thought and decided the time had come to take a stand. That's why I decided to conduct their wedding."

"You told us in your interview that you didn't actually conduct a lesbian wedding, that you just said a prayer," Hank Withers pointed out.

"It was a bit more complex than that," Sam said. Hank Withers was starting to annoy him. He made a mental note not to recommend Hank for the new outreach committee.

"Whichever the case," Dan said, "we appreciate what you did."

Hank leaned toward Sam. "Don't tell Leonard and Wanda Fink you support gay marriage. They won't stop until they get you fired. They'll stop giving, too. We've had some knock-down, drag-out fights over that topic."

Sam glanced around for an axe handle he could use to beat Hank Withers into silence.

"We were under the impression the meeting supported marriage equality," Libby said.

"Oh, Lord, no," Hank said. "You can't ever get Quakers to agree on anything. We'll be fighting about it for the next twenty years."

Libby frowned. "Oh, my, I had no idea. I've grown rather weary of arguing about this topic."

"As have I," said Dan.

"Then you probably don't want to come to our church," Hank said, reaching for a piece of bread and slathering it with butter. "Say, this is really good bread. Now if you're looking for a church that has settled this issue, you might want to look for a Unitarian church."

"The Episcopalians are generally supportive," added Norma Withers.

No wonder Quaker meetings never grow, thought Sam.

"Our daughter dates a Unitarian minister," Libby said. "Before we visited your meeting, we had given some thought to trying them out. But we enjoyed our time with you, and had made up our minds to come back."

"Give it time," Hank said. "Look around." He glanced around the room. "Where did Bruno disappear to? I wonder what tonight's special is?"

Sam was desperate, his mind racing, trying to rekindle the Woodrums' interest in Hope Meeting.

"What I've always appreciated about Quakers," he said earnestly, or what he hoped passed for earnest, "is our regard for prophetic ministry. While we might not always agree on a given topic, we do acknowledge the freedom of other Friends to believe differently."

"Most of us anyway," Hank said. "But we've got some real

hardheads, too. You should have seen Wayne Newby when we switched hymnals a few years ago. You'd have thought it was the end of the world, the way he went on."

"Yes, but to his credit he only stayed away for a week and came to terms with it," Sam pointed out.

Hank laughed. "Is that what he told you, that he only stayed away for a week? Heck, he was gone for three months. He still complains about it if you give him half a chance."

Before Hank could inflict further damage, Bruno arrived to take their orders, then the Woodrums, Norma, and Barbara excused themselves to use the restroom.

Sam turned to Hank. "I thought we were trying to get them into the meeting. Why are you being so negative?"

"Just telling them the truth," Hank said. "No sense in pumping them full of sunshine only for them to discover we're not as perfect as they thought we were."

"Let's at least try to get them in the door first, so we'll have the opportunity to disappoint them."

When everyone returned to the table, Barbara and Libby discussed libraries, which moved into a conversation on favorite books, which led to a discussion about politics, with all of them agreeing their state legislature was the worst in the nation, and perhaps in the world, and most likely worse than any group of legislatures in the past or any legislative body to come. It was great fun, and had them in a fine mood by the time dinner wound to an end.

"Meeting starts at ten thirty, right?" Dan Woodrum asked Sam as they were leaving.

"That's right," Sam said.

"Who's speaking this Sunday?" Libby asked.

"I am."

"No, I mean who's talking about their hobby?"

"Wayne Newby is going to tell us about his model train collection," Norma Withers said.

Sam cringed.

"Hey, that's pretty neat," Dan Woodrum said. "I have a good friend, a retired neurologist, who's a model train enthusiast. I might invite him along."

While he was pleased the Woodrums planned to return, Sam feared that Hank Withers's passion for honesty was going to reduce their already depleted ranks to zero. And while he would take his victories wherever he found them, he was a bit discouraged that quilts and model trains were a bigger draw than sermons.

44

There were three visitors the next Sunday, not including the Woodrums, who were also present, but no longer considered visitors. One trip to a Quaker meeting was all it took for most meetings to place someone on a committee. At the start of worship, during the announcements, Hank Withers announced the limb committee would be holding a yard cleanup day the following Saturday, and asked Dan Woodrum, in front of God and everyone, to be in charge of the walnut subcommittee, picking up walnuts that had fallen, before people stepped on them and snapped their ankles and fell and broke their hips and died in abject misery.

The visitors had come to hear Wayne Newby's model train presentation; they were a retired neurologist and two of his friends, also enthusiasts. Sam had tinkered with the order of worship, changing the lineup so he could have the final word. So Wayne spoke first, but they peppered him with so many questions there was no time left for Sam to preach, which Sam suspected was their intent all along. Ruby Hopper, pleased to observe their increasing numbers and the growing interest in their lectures, asked Wanda Fink if she might prepare a brief homily on painting for the next Sunday, which she happily agreed to do. That is, as happily as Wanda Fink ever agreed to do anything, which is to say she grimaced and nodded her head.

Sam introduced himself to the visitors, who, though polite, seemed uninterested in him and returned to gabbing with Wayne as quickly as they could. He scouted around for someone to talk with, but everyone was engaged with someone else, even Barbara, who was yakking with Libby Woodrum about books. Any fascination they might have had with Sam had apparently faded. The new had worn off.

He made his way to his office, where he found Leonard and Wanda Fink studying the books on his shelves, searching for heresy. Fortunately, he had left his heretical books, the ones written by east coast Episcopalians, at his home office, so as not to alarm the congregation. The books in his meetinghouse office were written by former atheists who'd had near-death experiences and accepted Jesus and took up preaching in Baptist churches in Mississippi. He had lots of books about angels, and stories of miraculous cures involving children with cleft palates. Books no one could object to. Who wouldn't be happy about God healing a cleft palate, for crying out loud?

"Can I help you?" he asked the Finks.

"No, no," they said, scurrying from the office like cockroaches when the light came on.

He took off his sport coat and hung it on the coatrack, then strolled into the kitchen, where he found Ruby Hopper cutting slabs of pie and heaping them with ice cream, which improved his mood considerably.

"Sorry we ran out of time and you didn't get to preach," she said. "But look on the bright side. At least you won't have to write a sermon for next Sunday. You've already got one."

Well, there was that.

"Take some pie to our guests, Sam. They might have come here to hear about model trains, but let's see if we can't entice them to come back for nobler reasons."

"Yes, ma'am," Sam said.

"And Sam."

"Yes."

"Your discomfort this morning was obvious. I know you don't like these talks, and to be truthful, they seem odd to me, too. But I can't remember the last time we had three visitors, so let's be patient and see where this goes." She held up her finger. "Just listen for a moment."

He could hear the excited chatter of people.

"It's been a long time since I've heard that much talking in this place," Ruby said. "It's a good sign, don't you think?"

"I suppose so," Sam said grudgingly, reluctant to surrender the point. "But tell me, is Wanda Fink a good artist?"

"I don't know. Why do you ask?"

"You asked her to talk about painting next Sunday."

"Oh, no, not that kind of painting. She paints rooms. Very nicely, I might add."

What a flaky bunch of Quakers, he thought.

"Sam, do you believe God can work through anyone or anything?"

"Yes, I do."

"Then let's see if God can't work through these circumstances, even if they're a little, uh, unusual," Ruby said.

Though it was good advice, it nevertheless annoyed Sam, who preferred that God do his work in a manner more agreeable with Sam.

45

After meeting for worship, Ruby Hopper phoned her cousin Miriam Hodge. They chatted about family matters, then Ruby inquired about Harmony Friends Meeting.

"We've let go of Paul Fletcher, our pastor. He was a disaster. Our attendance is half of what it was when Sam was here, and our superintendent keeps sending us pastoral candidates who are utterly unsuitable. Other than that, all is well. How is life at Hope Meeting?"

"We're seeing a slight uptick in attendance. Barbara is a delight and seems genuinely happy to be here, but Sam seems distracted, even angry at times."

"That doesn't sound like Sam," Miriam said. "He was always cheerful when he was here. He would get frustrated now and then, but what pastor doesn't. I certainly wouldn't want the job."

"What it was like when Sam left? I know the circumstances weren't the best, but he'd been your pastor for almost fifteen years. Did you give him an opportunity to say good-bye to the congregation, or thank him for his ministry? In a public way?"

"No, we didn't. Some of our elders insisted he not be allowed back in the pulpit and the rest of us didn't push the matter. I'm sure individual members of the meeting thanked him, but we did nothing as a congregation."

"Perhaps it might be good for our meetings, and good for Sam, if you invited him back for a Sunday morning. Especially now that Paul Fletcher is gone. Let Sam preach a farewell message, show him a little appreciation, wish him luck. I think he needs, uh, what do they call it?"

"Closure?"

"Yes, closure," Ruby said. "He needs closure, so he can move forward."

Miriam raised the subject at that week's meeting of the elders' committee. With unprecedented swiftness, Harmony Friends had not only kicked Paul Fletcher to the curb, they had pitched Dale, Fern, Bea, and Opal off the committee, replacing them with Deena Morrison, Asa Peacock, Judy Iverson, and Uly Grant, who immediately agreed with Ruby's proposal.

"We should have done this last year," Uly said.

"Let's have a dinner for them, too," said Deena. "I can head it up."

"I'll help," Judy Iverson said.

"What about the Friendly Women's Circle?" Asa Peacock asked. "Aren't they usually in charge of dinners?"

"If we ask them to do it, then Fern, Bea, and Opal will take it over. Quite frankly, I don't trust them," Miriam said.

Miriam thought for a moment. "You know what would be really nice? If we not only invited Sam and Barbara to return for a proper good-bye, but if we asked the people at Hope Meeting to join us. It'll show Sam we're happy for him and we'll be reaching out to a fellow Quaker meeting in the process. What do you think?"

Uly Grant said, "I'll supply the drinks and the cups."

It took them an hour to work out the details, then Miriam placed a quick phone call to Ruby Hopper, who gave her quick assent.

"Please don't tell Sam and Barbara about your meeting attending," Miriam advised. "Let's have it be a secret."

"A secret it will be," Ruby promised. "And our meeting will supply all the desserts."

A date was for the Sunday after next, and that evening Ruby phoned the entire membership of Hope Friends Meeting, told them of the news, warned them to keep it quiet, then put Hank Withers in charge of transportation, arranging the car pools.

"Always wanted to see inside the Harmony meetinghouse," he said. "It was built on the Akron plan, you know. Drawn up by an architect named Jacob Snyder for a Methodist Episcopal Church in Akron, Ohio, back in the 1870s. Quite an ingenious use of space."

When Hank Withers got cranked up about architecture, nothing held him back, so Ruby excused herself when he paused to breathe. She phoned Ellen Hadley, the clerk of the pie committee, to get her busy on the desserts.

It fell to Miriam Hodge to phone Sam and invite him to return to Harmony for a farewell sermon.

"That's not necessary," he said. "We've made the separation, no need to belabor it."

"We didn't get to give you a proper good-bye, and we'd like to make it up to you."

Sam thanked her for the kind thought, but declined her offer. Desperate, she called Sam's mother, who phoned Sam and ordered him to show up at the Harmony meetinghouse two Sundays from then unless he wanted to be responsible for her dying from a broken heart.

Ruby Hopper was cleaning the meetinghouse when Sam arrived the next morning to work in his office.

"I've been invited to return to Harmony for a good-bye Sunday," he told her. "I tried declining, but my mother called and insisted I come and you know how mothers are."

Ruby feigned ignorance and told him she'd have to check with the others, but that it shouldn't be a problem, provided it was only one Sunday. Hank Withers had been itching to give a lecture on Frank Lloyd Wright; perhaps he would consent to go long and fill in Sam's sermon time, too. Ruby would ask him.

The following Sunday at Hope Meeting, Sam delivered a message on generosity, making a few oblique hints about the joy of supporting the Lord's work, then Wanda Fink gave a talk about various wall-painting techniques—stenciling, striping, sponging, and rag rolling. Wanda's lesson was well received, with several people standing at the end of worship confessing to sloth, vowing to begin long-delayed painting projects. They sang a hymn and Sam gave the closing prayer, asking for safe travels as they returned to their homes, and thanking God for the hands that had prepared that morning's coffee, which they were all free to stay and enjoy. There were nine visitors, all of whom remained afterward to chat with Wanda. Ruby announced that Sam would be gone the next Sunday, returning to his hometown for a visit, but that Hank Withers had agreed to bring a message on the history of architecture, which she was certain everyone would enjoy.

"Not that we don't enjoy your messages," she said, turning to Sam. "I didn't mean it that way. No offense intended."

"None taken," Sam said. He had grown used to the idea that the lectures given by various members of the meeting were a bigger draw than his sermons. It was kind of Ruby Hopper to pretend otherwise.

46

Sam took Monday off, visiting Charley Riggle at the hardware store to discuss pocketknives and why things weren't made in America. They chewed on politicians and CEOs for a while, which left them feeling invigorated. Then he stopped past Drooger's Food Center for milk and bread. Since Barbara had taken a full-time job, the grocery shopping had fallen to him. With the boys gone, their grocery bill had dropped in half. Sam was eating more fresh vegetables and fewer Cocoa Puffs. He felt better, but was still suspicious of vegetables and cheerfully pointed out to Barbara newspaper articles about people dying of E. coli poisoning from bad spinach. So far as he knew, Cocoa Puffs had never killed anyone. He spent a half hour in the Food Center reading the magazines, boning up on various celebrities, should their names arise in polite conversation.

He arrived home in time to clean the house and start supper, then went on Facebook to spy on his sons. Seeing pictures of his sons with strangers never failed to alarm him. He wondered about the strangers, where they were from, what their parents were like. The people in the Facebook pictures never looked like Quakers. They looked like people who no longer attended church and didn't seem to miss it. He recognized Levi's apartment in one of the pictures. There were beer bottles in the background. Empty. A distant relation of Sam's had been a drunkard, so he thought about that for a brief while, got himself worked up, then sent Levi a text message telling him to straighten up.

He'd been nervous as a cat since Miriam had phoned asking him to speak at Harmony Friends. While it would be nice to see certain people, he dreaded the thought of crossing paths with Dale Hinshaw and Fern Hampton again. He turned his mind toward his sermon, fiddling with the opening, thinking of an appropriate Scripture reading, considering various passages about returning sons, and thought of the Prodigal Son. But that son had left of his own volition and had gone to the city to sin, while Sam had been tossed out on his keister for no good reason. Then he recalled Jesus's advice to his disciples—*If anyone will not welcome you or listen to your words, leave that home or town and shake the dust off your feet.* That had a certain appeal to it. A rousing shaking-the-dust-off-his-feet sermon would let them know where he stood on matters. He read that Scripture aloud, but couldn't do it without yelling. As tempted as he was to use it, he decided instead to try the wise-as-a-fox-but-gentle-as-a-dove approach, a less volatile bit of Scripture also recommended by Jesus.

It took three days for Sam to write his sermon, nudging it into shape, getting in a few digs, but on the whole being charitable. He took Friday off and drove to Purdue to visit Levi and remind him of his Christian heritage. On Friday evening he went with Barbara to the movies. He was feeling magnanimous and let her pick the movie. It was about a woman dying of cancer whose husband and children had been unappreciative until she died, then had realized how wonderful she had been and felt bad for the rest of the movie. Barbara had sobbed through the entire movie and had become upset with Sam for falling asleep; she accused him of insensitivity.

"It's a movie. It's make-believe. How can I be insensitive about something that didn't happen?" he asked.

But it was the principle of the thing, Sam's indifference to a dying woman who had married an insensitive clod. They stopped at a Baskin-Robbins for ice cream, which mollified her somewhat, and by the time they reached home, she had settled down altogether and admitted the woman in the movie had been overly dramatic and even a bit of a whiner.

"To be honest," Barbara said, "I was kind of relieved when she died. She was starting to annoy me."

They left for Harmony Saturday morning, arriving at Sam's parents in time for lunch. Chili with grilled cheese sandwiches and milk, Sam's favorite meal after Cocoa Puffs. Sam and his father took naps afterward, his father stretched out in a recliner, Sam sprawled on the couch. Sam's mother and Barbara walked to the Legal Grounds Coffee Shop for nonfat mocha lattes and pumpkin muffins. They went to bed early, Sam and Barbara in his old bedroom, on a mattress of unclear origins, passed down from a long-deceased relative. It had been Sam's mattress as a child and had formed an even deeper trough in the middle than their mattress at home, causing Sam and Barbara to roll into one another, which led to something else, which led to squeaking, which led to his mother tapping on their door and asking if anything was the matter.

The sun rose in a clear blue sky the next morning, a glorious fall day, so they walked to the meetinghouse, arriving fifteen minutes before worship. The parking lot was full, and the streets around the meetinghouse were choked with cars.

"It looks like Christmas or Easter," his mother said. "Look at all these cars."

"Maybe I should stay out here and direct traffic," his father said, always looking for an excuse to get out of church. He was a pacer, not a sitter. A man of action. "Yes, I believe that's what I'll do. Wouldn't want any fights or road rage. You never know with traffic like this."

They heard the crowd while still outside, the throb of laughter and excited chatter inside the meetinghouse.

"That looks like Ruby Hopper's car," Barbara said.

"Can't be," Sam said. "She's leading worship at Hope this morning."

As they climbed the meetinghouse steps, Matt the Unitarian pastor fell into step beside them.

"Look who came slinking back into town," Matt said. "Good to see you, Sam."

"What are you doing here?" Sam asked, shaking Matt's hand.

"Heard you were going to preach, so I took the Sunday off, and here we are."

"If it weren't for you Unitarians, I'd still be working here," Sam said.

"Yeah, you know us, we're just troublemakers. But look at the opportunity we gave you to be prophetic. You'll go down in history as the first Quaker minister to perform a same-gender marriage. A hundred years from now, everyone will think you were a saint. You should thank us."

They entered the meetinghouse together and people began thronging around Sam and Barbara, welcoming them. The Iverson twins presented Barbara with a bouquet of flowers. The scent of chicken and noodles rose up through the floor grates. It was like a dream. Sam felt woozy.

"What in the world is going on?" he asked Miriam Hodge, who had materialized beside him.

"We've come to thank you for being our pastor," Miriam said. "And to wish you God's blessings in your new ministry at Hope."

"That's why we're here," Ruby Hopper said, appearing at Miriam's side.

And indeed they were, all of Hope Friends Meeting, even the Finks, who at the moment were supposed to have been hearing a lecture on architecture, but instead were clustered around Sam and Barbara in the Harmony Friends meetinghouse.

"The Unitarians are here, too," Matt said. "We closed down our church today and told everyone to come here. We wanted to thank you for sharing your ministry with us."

Chris and Kelly were there, the lesbians with gender-neutral names, who had been the calm and gracious center of this hurricane. They stepped forward and embraced Sam and thanked him for his compassion on their special day.

"Now this is your special day and we wanted to be with you," Chris said.

"We very much appreciate what you did for us," Kelly added. "Sometimes it takes real bravery to be kind. We are grateful for your courage."

"I was happy to do it," Sam said. "It was an honor."

"Let's worship," Miriam said, taking Sam and Barbara by the arms and guiding them down front to the facing bench. "Sit up here in your old place. Barbara, you sit with him. We want to honor you, too."

Everyone took their seats, sliding over and making room. It was tight, but everyone fit. They entered into silence, their heads bowed. Sam peered around the room. Almost everyone he knew and loved was there. Looking at them, he felt something release inside him, a stone of resentment lodged in his spirit, breaking free.

One by one, out of the silence, people stood to speak, thanking Sam for all he had done for them. Ralph Hodge, recalling his long struggle with alcohol and how Sam had stood by him, driving him to AA all those years ago. Jessie Peacock reminding the congregation how Sam had rushed to the hospital when Asa had had his heart attack. She didn't mention it had taken three days for Sam to get there. No need to bring that up. Harvey Muldock rose to his feet and thanked Sam for his ministry to their family when they discovered their son was gay.

"We appreciate that you didn't judge him," Harvey said. "It meant a lot to us."

After Harvey spoke, Hank Withers gave a brief lecture on the Akron church design. Others stood, recalling their history with Sam and Barbara. It was like leafing through a picture album. Reminiscing and laughing and treasuring. It went on and on. When it came time to preach, Sam dispensed with his notes and thanked all present, even Dale and Fern, who admitted they had gone a little overboard and that if Sam wanted to come back and be their pastor, they wouldn't mind.

Then Miriam Hodge invited the members of Hope Friends Meeting to come forward and asked Sam and Barbara to stand before the congregation. She took Sam and Barbara by the hand and thanked God for their lives, then passed them along to Ruby Hopper and the people of Hope, who thanked God for bringing Sam and Barbara to them, then everyone said amen and Sam began to bawl and only stopped when Miriam said it was time to go downstairs and eat. She asked Sam to offer a meal blessing, which he did, with great enthusiasm.

He thanked God for chicken and noodles and the hands that prepared them, that rolled out the dough, that cut the noodles, that boned out the chicken, that laid out the noodles to dry. He thanked God for Chris and Kelly and wished them a happy future, and asked God to bless all the marriages of everyone, then thanked God for various people who had died, but were looking down on them from heaven at that very moment and were no doubt pleased by their reconciliation. Then, unsure how to wind up the prayer, he thanked God that they lived in a free country where people could worship as they wanted, or not worship, whichever the case may be. Then Barbara squeezed his hand, he stopped blabbering, and looked up just as Bob Miles took their picture for the *Harmony Herald*. They went downstairs and ate chicken and noodles, mashed potatoes, green beans, and yeast rolls, with pies for dessert, freshly baked by Ellen Hadley and the Hope Friends Meeting pie committee.

It was the best day Sam had ever had, even better than his wedding day, when he'd been so nervous he'd vomited on his grandmother in the receiving line. The day felt like a movie, like the final scene in *It's a Wonderful Life*, when the townspeople came to George Bailey's house and gave him money to save his bank, and sang "Auld Lang Syne."

They stayed afterward to help wash dishes and clean up, pausing now and again to hug people and wish them well. Finally, it was down to them and Ellis and Miriam Hodge, who walked all the Gardners home, where Sam and Barbara climbed in their car, waved good-bye, and headed toward Hope.

47

They heard from both their boys that evening. Levi called just before supper to ask for money, and Addison phoned from Fort Sill to tell them he was alive, that basic training was going well, that everyone was nice to him, especially his drill sergeant, and joining the army was the best decision he'd ever made.

"Is the drill sergeant standing next to you?" Sam asked. "If he is, ask how Grandma is doing."

"How's Grandma?" Addison asked.

"Did he tell you to say you were okay? If he did, ask about Grandpa?"

"How's Grandpa?" Addison asked.

"If you want us to break you out, ask to speak to your brother."

"Can I talk to Levi?" Addison asked.

Sam covered the mouthpiece with his hand and said to Barbara, "They're holding him against his will. He wants us to come get him."

"Let me talk to him," Barbara said, taking the phone from Sam.

"Hi, honey. Joining the army was your idea, not ours. We are not driving eight hundred miles to rescue you, so suck it up."

Just a year ago, she had wept when they had deposited their older son at college. Moaning and wailing and gnashing her teeth. Gone was the sentimental mother and wife, replaced by a stern librarian who brooked no nonsense, who whipped recalcitrant males into shape with a snap of her fingers.

My Lord, Sam thought, *she's become Miss Rudy.*

Miss Rudy, the former Harmony librarian, had single-handedly held off a siege of the town council bent on cutting her funds. She had locked the library doors and hid the only key in her bra, living on water from the toilet tank after the town had shut off water to the building to drive her out. She ate paste to keep up her strength. Oh, they had underestimated her. On the fourth day, the men of the council had capitulated, apologizing for cutting the funds, begging her to open the doors and come out. But she had stayed in the library an extra day, just to show them one could live on books, then marched out at noon on the fifth day, her head held high, and three pounds heavier. She had gained weight! When word got out, her picture made the cover of *American Libraries* magazine. Admiring letters poured in from librarians around the world—beaten down, beleaguered librarians who had drawn strength from her bravery. She answered each one in flowing, Palmer-method, handwritten script.

Sam looked at Barbara, as if seeing her for the first time.

"You've become Miss Rudy," he said.

"And don't you forget it, buster," she said.

Sam had always gotten along well with Miss Rudy. In fact, he had always admired strong women. Strong men annoyed him, because of their tendency to confuse arrogance for strength. But strong women, well, strong women intrigued him.

Later that evening, after a brief interlude of pleasant activity, Sam studied their bedroom ceiling.

"That was some morning," he said.

"Yes, it was," Barbara said, snuggling closer.

Snuggling! A strong woman who snuggled. Sam was woozy with adoration, and fell to sleep, for the first time in a long time, looking forward to life.

Turn the page for a preview
of the next novel in Philip Gulley's Hope series

A Lesson in Hope

**CENTER
STREET**

Available from Center Street in 2015,
wherever books are sold.

1

Sam Gardner had been the pastor of Hope Friends Meeting a scant four months when Olive Charles, aged ninety-eight, drew her last ragged breath and expired. On the four occasions Sam had spent at Olive's bedside, she hadn't said a word. She had appeared dead then, in fact. So when the funeral home had phoned Sam at 6 a.m. on a Monday, his day off, to report her demise, he hadn't been at all surprised. Her funeral had been a small one. She had never married, but did have one niece in Chicago whom she hadn't seen in forty years, who'd showed up at the funeral bawling her eyes out at the sight of Olive lying stiff in her casket, but had recovered quickly, pulled Sam aside, and asked him if the will had been read.

"I have no idea," he'd told her.

"Do you know if Aunt Olive had any other relatives? I'd kind of lost touch with the family. Did anyone ever come visit her at the nursing home?"

"Just me and folks from the meeting," Sam said.

"Did she say anything about money?"

"Not to me, but then she'd stopped talking about a year ago."

"We were very close," the niece said. Sam hadn't caught her name—Ramona, Regina, Rowena, he wasn't sure—and after only five minutes with her had no interest in learning it.

The following Sunday morning at meeting for worship, Ruby Hopper talked about Olive and showed slides from their vacations.

"Olive was one of our founding members," Ruby said, by way of introduction. "Very kind. Very dedicated to the meeting. We vacationed together until three years ago, when her health turned. She was an absolute joy."

"Smart, too," Hank Withers said. "She was on the building committee when they hired me to design it. She would have made an excellent architect."

Hank was a retired architect and thought it high praise indeed that Olive could have been similarly employed.

Olive's attorney had phoned the meetinghouse office two days later, early in the morning, to inform Sam that Olive had left to her beloved Quaker meeting her entire estate, consisting of one house and its contents, a 1979 Ford Granada with four snow tires, barely used, and a bank account a dab north of eight hundred thousand dollars. Sam had never cared for lawyers, but in that moment he felt a general warmth toward the profession and probably would have hugged the man had they been in the same room.

Ramona, or Regina, or whatever her name was, phoned a few minutes later, screeching about suing the church and everyone in it and coming down there and getting what was rightfully hers, since she'd been the only one who'd ever loved Olive. Sam let her rant a little while, then hung up the phone.

Sam Gardner loved nothing more than to be in possession of a juicy morsel of news no one else knew, so he savored the situation for several minutes, sitting in the quiet of his office, then phoned the members of the church, summoning them to an emergency meeting that evening. He couldn't tell them over the phone. He had to tell them in person, all at once, so they would hear the same thing. He would see them at seven.

"Should I bring a pie?" Ruby Hopper asked.

"Several," Sam said. "Can you make one of those apple pies with the crumbly things on top?"

"A Dutch apple pie? I certainly can."

It was shaping up to be the finest day Sam Gardner had ever had in thirty years of ministry.

Barbara was at work, at Hope Elementary, where she served as the librarian. Sam walked the five blocks there, caught her in between classes, and told her what had happened.

"That's two hundred thousand dollars a visit," he pointed out. "Not bad for an hour's work."

"Sure beats library pay," Barbara said.

"Her niece is madder than a wet hen. She called to tell me she's going to sue the meeting and everyone in it."

"This is the niece who hadn't seen her in forty years?" Barbara asked.

"That's the one."

"They come out of the woodwork when they sniff a little money, don't they?"

Sam was too distracted to work on his sermon, so he spent the rest of the day fending off curious church members who happened to be in the neighborhood and dropped in to visit.

"Is the yearly meeting going to throw us out?" Wilson Roberts asked. "They better not, that's all I can say. Not five years ago I donated a brand-new toilet and sink for the superintendent's office. They throw us out and I'm going over there and taking them back."

"No, the yearly meeting isn't throwing us out," Sam said.

"Then why did you call a meeting?"

"You'll find out tonight, along with everyone else. I don't want to have to tell the story a dozen different times. You'll have to be patient, Wilson."

When Wilson realized he couldn't wear Sam down, he took his leave. No sooner had he gone than Wanda and Leonard Fink stopped past. Sam's phone call had wakened them; they had been speculating ever since and had concluded that Sam had become an atheist and was announcing his resignation, which didn't trouble them in the least. Indeed, they were relieved, and not at all surprised, ever since they had seen a book on his office shelves titled *The Pastor's Secret: The Rise of Doubt Among Clergy.*

"We know what the meeting is about," Wanda Fink said, cutting to the chase.

They probably do, the big snoops, Sam thought.

"I would prefer not to discuss it right now," Sam said. "I want to tell it only once."

"I never thought I would live to see the day when something like this would happen," Leonard said. "Have you given any thought to what this will do to our church?"

"I've been thinking of nothing else," Sam said. "It will be a test for us, that's for sure. But I prefer not to say anything more until tonight, when everyone is present."

"How can you sit there and be so calm?" Wanda said. "It's like you don't even care."

"I care a great deal. I just don't think it's anything to get all worked up about. It's happened to other churches and they dealt with it. So will we."

"We? What do you mean we? You're not planning on staying, are you?"

"I most certainly am," Sam said. "The meeting needs steady leadership at a time like this."

Wanda and Leonard stormed from the office. As long as he lived, Sam would never be able to figure out some people.